PLAIN GIRL

by Virginia Sorensen

MIRACLES ON MAPLE HILL
(NEWBERY MEDAL WINNER)

PLAIN GIRL

VIRGINIA SORENSEN

Illustrated by Charles Geer

HARCOURT BRACE & COMPANY

San Diego   New York   London

Library of Congress Cataloging-in-Publication Data
Sorensen, Virginia Eggertsen, 1912–
Plain girl.
Summary: Despite her father's objections, a young
Amish girl secretly looks forward to attending public
school where she makes a best friend and gains a new
perspective on her family's way of life.
[1. Amish — Fiction. 2. Schools — Fiction.
3. Friendship — Fiction.] I. Geer, Charles, ill.
II. Title.
PZ7.S72Pl   1988   [Fic]   87-46190
ISBN 0-15-262437-6

Printed in the United States of America

GHIJK

FOR ANNA MARIE SMITH
*and with warm gratitude to Anna Beckstine,
who first told me the story of a Plain Girl.*

CONTENTS

PLAIN GIRL

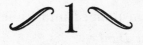

1

ESTHER

"Esther!"

Esther jumped in surprise. Mother's voice was not usually so loud. She came hurrying into the garden, where Esther had just finished picking corn. "Here, I will take them in," she said, and held out her full black skirt for the fresh ears to be dumped into it. "Now you may go and gather eggs for supper."

She did not say what fine big ears Esther had picked, as she usually did, or even seem to notice. Before she disappeared into the kitchen she called back, "I left the egg-basket out by the chicken coop."

Well, Esther thought, something was the matter. Unless Mother and Aunt Ruth had made fifty puddings since noon there were plenty of eggs in that house for a dozen suppers. They had not made puddings at all, as she knew, but apple pies for which no eggs were needed.

Somebody must be at the house just now, somebody Mother did not want her to see.

As always, whenever anything out-of-the-way happened, a question jumped into Esther's mind: *Was it something about Dan?*

Before she was halfway to the chicken coop, she knew at least part of the trouble. An automobile stood by the front gate. Two strange men without any hats on their heads at all, or any beards on their chins, sat in the seat, looking toward the house. She hurried inside with the hens and closed the door quickly behind her. But she went at once to the wired opening across the front and looked out.

It was a shining black car with a colored picture painted on the door. There were words too, but she could not read them so far away. They were not huge words like the ones she saw on cars sometimes when she went to market with Father and Mother, like POTATO CHIPS, HANDY LAUNDRY, DRINK OBERT'S ORANGY ORANGE! If these two men had something to sell, Esther thought, they'd as well drive away before Father came out of the barn. Father knew exactly what things he needed and where to get them. Besides, Esther knew, he wasn't going to like an automobile sitting right in front of his own gate.

The barn door opened. Father came out. On Father anger showed very plainly because it almost never happened to him. Now his beard looked so stiff and fierce

4

that he did not seem like Father at all. Esther stood so
quiet inside the coop that the chickens forgot she was
there and began to peck about her shoes. Surely, now
those men saw Father looking as he did, they would
drive away.

But they did not. Instead, one of them opened the
door and leaned out and called, "Mr. Lapp?"

Father nodded. Once. He did not move toward them
one single step. It was as if he said, "If they want to
speak with me they can do the walking. It isn't as if
I wanted to speak to *them*."

"Oh, dear," Esther thought. "I wish they would go
away." Now Father would not say a single word at
supper and so neither would Mother. Aunt Ruth
would not dare to speak, then, and of course a little
girl never spoke unless she was spoken to. It would
be as bad as it had been right after Dan went away.

But the men did not leave. Instead they both
climbed out of the car and came through the gate
and straight toward where Father stood. The first
man carried a paper in one hand, reading as he
walked. When he came close to Father, he looked up
and said, "I understand you have a daughter, Esther
Lapp?"

Esther jumped from the window so quickly that

the chickens at her feet flew in every direction, squawking. Then she stood still, against the door.

"Yes," she heard Father say. "I have a daughter Esther."

The man cleared his throat. Now the chickens huddled together, very still under the perches, and Esther crept forward toward the window again.

"From our records, we find that she is almost ten years old," the man said. Esther could see his face quite well now, looking very pink without any beard, like a young unmarried man. Yet he was old, for his clipped hair was gray over his ears. "Why hasn't she ever been to school?"

So it was that. They had seldom spoken of it, but Esther had heard what was said when Ruth first came to help in the house and give her lessons. Father had known it might happen. Now here it had come. But his voice sounded very clear and steady and she saw how straight and proud he stood under his broad stiff-brimmed hat.

"We have taught Esther here at home," he said. "She is able to read and write very well now. In English. And in German too."

"That may be so," the man said, and glanced at his companion. "But it happens, Mr. Lapp, that we have a compulsory school law in Pennsylvania. I'm sure

7

you remember—we have talked about this matter be-fore."

"Quite some time ago now," said the other man. "Before, I believe, the trouble was about your son." He looked at the paper in his companion's hand. "Our records show that you were arrested and fined three times before he finally went to school. Daniel Lapp. Isn't that your son?"

Father did not answer, and Esther began to tremble from her head to her toes. The name *Daniel* was never mentioned in that house or in that yard or any place where Father might happen to hear it. She herself had heard him say, right after Dan had gone away, "We will not speak of Daniel here again."

The strange man did not know that. He even *re-peated* the name, looking straight into Father's face. "You finally sent Daniel to school, and he finished," the man said. "We understood you meant to send your daughter without trouble when the time came."

"Esther is learning here at home," Father said slowly in a heavy stubborn voice. "We Amish people believe in the law; you should know it. But we do not believe in a bad law that forces men to send their children to learn bad ways. We are able to teach our children everything they will need to know here on the farm."

A silence fell. Only the chickens moved around

Esther's skirt, looking stiff-legged and pop-eyed and silly.

"Believe me, Mr. Lapp, we're sorry about this," the first man said. "But until you people provide a good school of your own—one the Superintendent can approve, mind you—every Amish child must go to the school provided. The one in this neighborhood is a very good school; my own boy goes there. This fall we have a splendid teacher—"

"It is not the teachers that are bad," Father said.

Again the silence. They seemed to know what Father had meant to tell them, and looked awkwardly at each other. It was not that the teachers were bad, or the school, or the children. It was only that there were so many different children at the school, with different ways and different clothes. So many different things put strange ideas into an Amish head sometimes. It had happened to Dan; Father was afraid it would also happen to Esther.

The first man broke the silence in a determined voice, looking at the paper and speaking his words as if he read them out. "We are to inform you, Mr. Lapp, that your daughter Esther must be in school from the age of eight until she is seventeen. Her case has been overlooked too long already." He glanced at Father's fierce beard, which stood out upon the air when his head was held so high. "The only excuse provided by law, Mr. Lapp, is dire financial need—" His glance swept over the neat farm and the great barn and the strong house, and Esther knew he was thinking there was no need here or ever would be.

Father turned his back. The other man spoke then, in a determined way, clearing his throat at the beginning like a preacher about to begin his sermon. "On September the 8th, next week," he said, "the school bus will come along this road. If your daughter does not appear, Mr. Lapp, you will be arrested before night."

Father had started for the barn while he talked. Suddenly he stopped short and spoke over his shoulder. "Esther will not ride in the school bus," he said. "That is not in the law. I will take her back and forth myself!"

He disappeared. The barn door closed quietly after him. No matter how angry Father might be, he would never slam a door.

"Well!" the first man said.

The two stood for a moment, looking around. "You have to admit they're wonderful farmers," one of them said. "Look at those fields. And never a machine on the place."

His companion nodded and they began to walk back

toward the gate. "All the Plain People are good farmers," one of them said. "I wish we had as many here as they do in Lancaster County. They're all rich, the best farmers in the world and they know it."

"They're not afraid of hard work," said the other man. "Only of school."

They laughed and got into the car again. To turn it around they had to drive it into the yard and back it up. Esther could see the picture quite clearly for a minute, a blue design like a shield. She could read the words too: THE COMMONWEALTH OF PENNSYLVANIA.

Father came out of the barn again, looking at the cloud of dust the car left behind it on the road. Esther felt sorry about how he felt. But about going to school—she was not in the least sorry for that. Gathering the eggs while the chickens fluttered and scolded her, she told herself the truth. Dan had loved the school and now she was glad that she would see the wonderful things he had described to her. Books with colored pictures on every page. Bright crayons and chalk and paper to fold and cut. Pictures on the walls, curtains at the windows made of paper with crinkly edges. That wonderful little machine that brought music out of little black plates by scratching with a needle . . .

So many things! She was so excited she stumbled

over the doorsill and almost spilled the eggs. She had passed the schoolhouse many times when she was with Father and Mother, in the wagon. Crowds of children laughed and played and ran together, tossing balls.

In the yard near the house she stood still, looking in the direction of the school. Sometimes in the winter she had heard the bell ringing from its little white tower. On a clear cold day she could hear it very well over the fields and the meadows.

If only Father did not mind so much! she thought.

2

A NIGHT VISITOR

At supper it was just as Esther had expected. Father did not speak of the strangers who had come, or of the school, or of anything else. He prayed in silence before and after supper, and then he went out to the barn again.

"The calf is not well," Mother said, watching Father anxiously as he disappeared through the big painted doors. Esther knew that Father went out there because he wanted to be alone.

Esther helped with the dishes and swept up the crumbs on the floor. But there wasn't much to do. Since Mother's young sister Ruth had come to visit, after Dan went away, and then stayed and stayed and stayed, the work seemed always done. Aunt Ruth was a wonderful housekeeper, as Mother herself was. Now there was always a cupboardful of pies. Except when church was held here, the pies never entirely disappeared as they used to when Dan was at home.

"What an appetite!" Mother used to say with a

proud laugh, looking up at Dan who stood almost as high as the top of a door.

Tonight Mother and Ruth did not talk much either. Usually they chattered endlessly, about gardens and cooking and hens and lambs and babies. Or about what had been sold at a farm-sale in the neighborhood, and at what bargain prices. Or about where church had been held last week and where it would be held the next. Or about a Sing in somebody's barn on Saturday night, or an apple-paring on Wednesday. Until recently, they often talked about a quilting for a bride. Or about what girls might be married in November.

Nobody had said so, but now it would not do to speak of the quiltings and the marriages. Esther knew this without being told. The sad look on Ruth's face told it all without words.

When the work was finished, Ruth went out as she often did lately and sat on the back porch with her knitting. Even as the dusk gathered she could go on with her stitches, so nobody ever thought she was sitting out there wasting her time.

"Aunt Ruth," Esther said in a low voice, and sat very near as she loved to do, "did you see the men who came today?"

For a long moment Ruth seemed not to hear. She

looked out toward the barn and over the wide fields and along the road, keeping her fingers busy and counting with her lips how many stitches she was making. At last she stopped counting and said gently, "Yes, Esther, I saw them."

"You said you went to school where you lived," Esther said.

"Yes," Ruth said again. "That was a long way from here, but it was still Pennsylvania. We had the same laws there."

"Mother went to school too," Esther said.

Ruth counted again for a time, and then she spoke slowly as she did when she was explaining something in a lesson. "It was different there, Esther, because there were many Amish in that neighborhood. We had a school of our own. When I go back again, I am going to study, I think, and learn to be a teacher myself. We need more Amish teachers; you've heard the preacher say so."

She had stopped knitting entirely and looked so sad and lonesome as she spoke of going away that Esther instantly had a lump in her throat. "You know enough to be a good teacher already," she said. "All those letters you taught me! Did you know, Ruth, that I am almost through with both *Genesis* and *Exodus?*"

"You do very well," Ruth said. She smiled. "You won't need to worry about school. You'll be able to read as well as anyone there."

But even her smile looked sad. Esther knew why Ruth did not want to go away again, even to her own home where she had lived a very happy life until she was eighteen. It was because of Hans.

"Maybe you can come back here and start a school

for us," Esther said eagerly. "Then it will be the kind
of school Father wants."

Ruth reached out and pressed her hand. "Perhaps
I can," she said. Then, quickly, she began to knit
again. There seemed nothing more to say. Lately it
had become harder and harder to talk to Ruth. When
she had first come she had been eager and gay and full
of laughter; she never sat like this, in the dusk. Was it
always like that, Esther wondered, when a girl grew
up and had to think about young men? She was glad
she was only starting to be ten and didn't have to be in
love. Love seemed to be the trouble every time when
a girl looked sad. Sarah Yoder looked even sadder than
Ruth last Sunday, sitting after church in this very
place. When Esther happened to come out of the
house, she had asked suddenly, "Esther, hasn't your
Mother heard from Daniel at all?"

It was good Father hadn't heard her ask such a thing.
Before Esther had time to shake her head, even, he had
come outside with the men.

Poor Sarah! Everybody had known she liked Daniel
more than she liked any other boy. And that he liked
her most of all the girls. People often laughed and
teased them, for Dan always sat beside her after the
Sings and she was the one he took home in his buggy,
every time.

But he did not love her very much, after all, surely. Or would he have gone away? Now, even in meeting, Sarah looked as sad and as lonesome as Ruth did this minute, clicking her needles and counting stitches and looking at the rising moon. Hans had not gone away, of course, but then he had not come to see Ruth here at the house, either. Quite often, Esther had seen him driving his buggy past, along the road, but he had not come and turned the light of his buggy into Ruth's room at night the way a young Amish man does when he wants to marry a girl. Now it was beginning to be September and Ruth must go back home, and the month for being married—which was November—was not very far away.

Last Sunday, after meeting, Father had looked directly at Hans during supper. "Only one woman can make pies as well as my own wife," Father had said, "and that is her sister Ruth."

Everybody had laughed but Ruth herself, who blushed and turned away. Esther did not know whether Hans laughed, because he lowered his head over his plate.

What Father had said was true; he would not have said it otherwise. Besides being able to cook, Ruth had a huge chest at home, Esther knew, all carved with birds and flowers; it was filled to the top with beautiful things Ruth herself had made.

"It is time for bed now, Esther," Mother called from the house.

Esther stood up at once. "Good night," she said.

"Good night. I'll be coming soon," Ruth answered. She looked up with a smile. "Esther, if you're afraid about school, we will work on those letters again before I go."

But it was not about the letters Esther thought, when she lay in her bed in the dark. Perhaps the school would not be pleasant, after all, in a place where she must go alone. Perhaps it would be the way it was in town sometimes when people turned their heads to watch, looking and nudging each other and saying, "Look! There are some of those Plain People!" In town, Father was often the only man in sight who wore a wide-brimmed hat and had no buttons on his coat. Mother was the only woman in a long dress with a black apron and a black prayer-cap. Would the children look at her, too, and nudge each other, she wondered, and whisper behind their hands?

She began to wish she did not have to go to school, after all. For Father to be arrested, as the strange man said—what did it mean? Perhaps it meant that he would have to hire a lawyer and stand up in a court, the way he had to do before, about Dan and the school-law. She heard Father coming in from the barn at last; he said only "Good night," and came up the stairs. Then Mother came with Ruth.

Ruth came into the room quietly, thinking that Esther was asleep long since. She undressed with the tiniest rustlings in the dark and knelt to say her prayers. Then she lay down in her bed on the other side of the room.

Across the hall in the room he shared with Mother, Father began to talk. Now that he thought everybody was asleep, he could speak as he wished to Mother alone. He talked on and on, Mother making only her low little "Yes" and her low little "No, no!" Once Esther heard the word "school," so she knew for sure they were talking about her, and about the strange men, and about the law.

She could not remember the trouble about Dan and the school, for she had not even been a baby then, at the very beginning. She had still been in heaven. But she knew they had postponed Dan's going until there was a lot of trouble and until he was the biggest boy in the room. She knew, too, that Father and Mother believed the things Dan learned had made him go away.

But they did not need to be afraid about *her*, Esther

thought, filled with love as she heard their familiar voices in the night. Never in the world would she go away from home, from Father and Mother who were always kind and always worked so hard from morning until night to make life good here on the farm. This was her own place, this room in this house with wide fields and the beautiful woodlands around it. Fire burning in the stove and the good smells of baking meat and Sunday pies. The huge barn and all the pleasant animals. The music and talk of meetings and sings, and young people laughing together. All the long row of yellow-topped buggies, winding along the road to church on Sunday morning, or to a wedding perhaps in November, or to a funeral. The People were always alike, wherever they went, in their simple clothes. She knew every single one of them here, by name and by face and by all their special ways. From behind, of course, one couldn't be told from another. But by their faces she knew every single one.

She must tell Father she would never think of going away. Never, never as long as she lived. Where would she go? The idea of going anywhere alone filled her with terror; she shivered and drew the covers tight against her chin.

"The first day of school, when he is taking me there

in the buggy," she thought, "I will tell Father I will never go away."

At last there was silence everywhere. She fell asleep. Then, suddenly, she was stark awake again. The moon was shining brightly into the room, onto the wall. But no. No, it was not the moon! It was not a soft radiance over everything, like moonlight, but a direct beam that made a single spot on the clean white wall.

Ruth was sitting up, gazing at the light. "Oh, God bless us, God bless us, Esther!" she whispered, as if she had begun to say her prayers all over again.

Esther was sitting up too, and saw Ruth get out of bed and run to the window. It was like a strange dream. Ruth flung the window wide to the night and spoke out of it. "Yes! Yes, I am coming down!" she called. Her teeth were chattering, but she laughed and turned as if she were dancing and leaned down and kissed Esther upon the mouth. "Go back to sleep now, my dear," she said. "Esther, do you know it is Hans out there? He has come for me!"

How beautiful Ruth looked, there in the light in her white nightgown, laughing, her hands trembling. Her hair was hanging down to her waist and she gathered it up and tucked it under her cap properly. She put on her clothes as if it were day again already. Esther heard her go into the hall and knew how she must feel her way down the dark stairs. A door opened and closed again. Then voices, at first excited and then gradually quiet. Hans' voice. Then Ruth's voice. Like Father's and Mother's earlier, turn and turn about, but mostly Hans did the talking and Ruth said, "Yes, yes." Esther knew without hearing the words. Not one sound came from her parents' room; in the morning they must pretend to be surprised to find Hans there.

Now, Esther thought, there would be a wedding in this very house. Then Ruth would go away, but she would not be sorry to go now, because she would be going with Hans, her sweetheart. For the rest of the night they would make their plans. They would decide when to announce their coming marriage. They would decide on which Tuesday or which Thursday in November they would have their wedding. They would decide what relatives they would go to visit, first, second, third. They would talk about building a house and where they would live until it was finished.

Esther could hardly wait until it should be light and time to go down. At breakfast there would be laughter and happiness today, and all the plans would be told.

Some day— The thought was so strange and wonderful that Esther sat up in bed again. Some day when she had finished at the school and had filled a huge carved chest with things she had made, somebody would come and shine a light into this same window for *her*. *Whoever would it be?* Somebody short and plump like Hans? No, no. Somebody tall and hand-some and full of gay spirits and laughter. Like Dan . . .

She lay down again, for the nights were getting cooler lately, but she was not sleepy in the least. It wasn't of Ruth she was thinking now, but only of Dan. At school, he had said, he was called Dan instead of Daniel, and liked it very much. She had called him Dan when they were alone; that was one of their secrets together. Now it was always as Dan that she thought of him.

Why couldn't he have stayed here at home until he could go with Sarah, who loved him? He could have gone, then, to a fine new house on the place Father had planned he should have for his own. All the People would have been singing and laughing and playing games at his wedding, and his old friends would have tossed him over the fence. Father would have smiled, and Mother, and everybody, and they could all pay visits after the wedding, back and forth.

How was it for Dan now? How had it been to go?

And where? How? Often Esther seemed to be speaking to him. Among what people do you sing now, Dan, with your big voice? Who hears you laughing? Who cares what you eat, and what you wear, and whether you are warm enough when you go to bed at night?

3

WHAT HAPPENED TO DAN

Some people come and go and it never matters very much, except, of course, to the few who love them in their family. But when Dan came or went, everybody noticed. It was good to see him come into a door, filling it up and then towering in the room. Esther always loved to see people turn and look at him when he came. Mother always looked proud and smiled as she lowered her eyes, not wishing to show how proud she was. Every time Father prayed that he might remain simple and humble, Esther wondered whether he was thinking of how proud Daniel had made him feel every day.

All Plain Men prayed against Pride. Every Sunday there was something in the sermons to warn women against Vanity.

Perhaps Dan had been too proud, Esther thought. His skin was clear, his cheeks pink and his hair bright yellow. When he spoke his voice boomed out, and when he sang— Sometimes, when he sang at meeting

Esther forgot to take her own part, it was so beautiful. But one day she had heard him singing out in the barn.

As Esther lay in her bed, waiting for dawn, she wondered if that had not been the beginning.

It was a different song and Dan's voice boomed out of the barn with it. It was a song never heard in any Amish house, here or anywhere. It had gay words to a gay tune, all about mockingbirds on a hill, singing in the morning. You would not imagine such a song could do more harm in the world than the birds themselves.

Esther saw Father listening. Then he marched out to the barn, and she ran after him to see what happened. "Where does that foolish song come from, Daniel?" Father asked.

Dan laughed. Even at the time, before there had been much trouble, Esther knew it was a mistake for Dan to laugh.

"From John's radio," he said. "He has permission to have a radio in his barn."

Dan did not need to remind Father about the radio. Everybody knew. Since a terrible storm came suddenly the year before, one radio was kept in the neighborhood so the People could learn in advance about the weather. Advice was given to farmers too, about planting and other matters to do with the farms. Every

Sunday evening, after the preaching, and sometimes at the market in town, the men stood around talking about whether the advice on the radio had been good that week, or bad.

Father always said it was bad, or else he said it told him nothing he had not learned long before from the Almanac.

"Daniel, the radio is not meant to hear music," Father said.

"Well, sometimes more than the weather will come while a man is milking a cow," Dan said.

Father told him never to sing the song again. He knew plenty of good songs to sing out of the *Ausbund*, the book used by the People for singing for nearly four hundred years.

When Esther heard Dan singing the song again, she shook in her skin until she saw that Father was away. Sometimes he sang it when Father was working far out in the fields. And not only the song about the mockingbirds came from the barn. There were other songs, one especially that had such a beautiful melody Esther caught herself thinking of the tune when she lay in bed at night. It said "I love! I love you! I love you!" over and over. Esther wondered whether Dan ever sang it to Sarah when he took her home from meeting in his buggy. Or if he did, whether Sarah would approve.

For a while before Daniel went away, he not only prayed in silence with the others, but ate in silence too. Before that he had talked and laughed, even when his mouth was full.

But in the fields, when he was working behind the horses, he tossed his head in the sun like a young colt. He often stopped plowing and looked at the sky.

One day she asked him, shyly, whether he was looking for mockingbirds. But he laughed and said, "No, Esther, of course not. Those birds live only where it is always warm. The year around, in some places," he added, "it is warm! Can you imagine such a thing?"

Of course she couldn't. But one day he showed her pictures of it, in a book he brought from school.

It was during the last few weeks he was at home, in mid-summer, over a year ago now, that she saw him in the middle of the day, simply lying at the edge of the field where the brook ran. He was chewing grass, pulling the sweet tips off with his teeth and throwing the heads away.

When he saw her coming, he said, "Esther, I'm lazy today. Nobody should work in such weather."

"It should be Sunday," Esther said, and looked at

the blue sky. For a weekday, it was working weather, the best working weather in the world.

Dan shook his head. "No. On Sunday it's harder work than ever, and all indoors." She knew he meant when the meetings were at their house, in their turn, and benches had to be carried in and out and tables set up. Esther had never thought of those things as work. Never before Dan said it. Afterward she knew it was part of the trouble. Singing those gay songs was the beginning. Father was right when he tried to stop it with the first song about the mockingbirds.

If that song had never come on John's radio, maybe Dan would never have gone away. Esther felt sure that Dan had, after that, a new feeling about the air. Not just the air going up and up but the air going on and on, around the world, blowing songs from one place to another. Far away, people were singing. Different people. Different songs. Once you thought about it you were already almost on your way.

Esther thought about it once because of Dan. It was like being a bird and she felt dizzy and came down quick and tried never to let the feeling come back. When the feeling started, she began quickly to think of things on the ground, of things like dishes to do or bread to mix or seeds to plant. A thought like that one about the air could be put away. It was possible to put something in front of it in your mind, like a platter in front of the sugar bowl.

One day she had been coming from a neighbor's house along the road. Dan had been at school all day. It was early spring, over a year ago. An automobile came behind her and she looked at the ground and moved far to the side to let it pass.

It did not pass. It stopped beside her and she looked up in surprise.

"Hello, Esther!" It was Dan getting out of the car. He said to the driver, "Thank you for giving me a ride. This is Esther, my sister."

It was a little rattling black car and Esther looked at it as it went on down the road. Two boys were in it, and one of them turned and looked at her with the same expression people had in town when they turned their heads to stare.

One of the boys in the car waved good-by. Dan waved back.

As she and Dan started walking together, Esther could not think of a word to say. Dan too walked in silence. Finally, near the home place, Dan stopped and said, "Tell Father if you feel you should. They are my best friends at school. I was walking home and they offered me a ride. I always wanted to see what one of those machines was like. Now I know."

She did not tell Father. She felt she should tell him, but she didn't. Afterward, of course, she knew she had made a mistake. When a preacher at a meeting said, as one did very often, never to make *The First Step Away,* she knew now what it was he meant. After Dan had gone away, she understood. Without the first step you could not make the second, the third, the final one that took you out of sight. You could never arrive at the house yonder if you never stepped from your own. It was very simple to stay at home.

A day came when Dan was walking with her on the street in town. Father was buying feed for the chickens. Dan looked at anybody who passed, Esther saw. He did not look either bold or shy as he looked, but curious. He looked even at girls. Then he said the strangest thing Esther ever heard in all her life. "I wonder," Dan said, "what harm a button may do a man's soul."

A *button?* At first she could not imagine what it was he meant by such a question. Coats were as well fastened with hooks and eyes. Aprons tied. And bonnets. But the question kept coming back into Esther's mind. What harm can a button do a man's soul? All people but the Plain People fastened clothes with buttons.

In the middle of a meeting one Sunday, soon after that, Esther's eyes would not leave the preacher's coat behind his Book. All smooth; no button anywhere.

33

What harm can a button do a man's soul? she thought. Such a question had never been asked in one of those meetings, she was sure. Or answered. It frightened her to be sitting among the People with such a question strong in her mind. She began to count how many had come, how many men, how many women, how many children, how many pies would be needed, anything to make her mind too busy to think about buttons. But even so, the question had kept slipping through her mind, between the numbers, like a little snake slipping under a stone.

She would never forget the supper after meeting that night. She had been helping to carry the food, and suddenly she heard Dan asking that question in front of them all. She did not dare to look at Father or at anybody. She stopped still with the platter of meat in her hands, looking at the floor. There was a silence, and everybody looked, then, at the preacher.

Preacher Stutzinger had been chosen by lot, having drawn a certain paper from the Bible on a chosen day. So it was known he was approved by God Himself.

"Well, Daniel," he said, "I've heard that buttons are good places for the Devil to hang onto!"

The men laughed, but it was not good hearty laughter, and they stopped laughing very soon.

"There are those who say buttons are made from the bones of animals, so are never used," the preacher said. "But we eat meat, and buttons may be made of wood. The reason I have heard given is that buttons are a decoration. They are to men as jewelry is to vain women." He looked around at the solemn faces. "Soldiers wear buttons," he said. "They polish them like medals!"

To Esther's relief, Dan nodded then and said, "It is a good reason." Dan might sing of love and mockingbirds, but he felt like Father and all the others about the wickedness of men fighting other men.

Everybody had begun to eat once more, and that question never bothered Esther in church afterward.

But then Dan had finished at the school. He could read anything he tried to read and knew many things about the world that he liked to tell Esther when nobody was about. If he was sorry to be through with school, it did not show in the least. Dan was lighthearted. A whole summer and a whole winter and another summer he stayed contentedly at home. Mother and Father laughed when he made such a large light on his buggy. According to the laws of Pennsylvania, every vehicle that moved on a road at night must have a light. "Well, Daniel, a light that big will be sure to wake a girl, no matter how sleepy," Mother said.

Esther had looked at Dan and said, "What girl? Sarah?"

But Dan shook his head, laughing. "Any girl who will have me!" he said.

Esther knew that any girl among the People would have Dan if he so much as nodded toward her. But especially Sarah. Sarah would have cared all her life what Dan ate and what he wore. She would have loved to listen to him laugh. And sing too, if only he could have been contented with the beautiful old songs.

But Dan never did shine the bright light of his buggy in Sarah's window, or any other girl's. Instead, he went away. It was about a year ago now, for it was full harvest-time, and there were signs along the road saying in tall red letters, COME TO WOODBORO FAIR. It was from the Fair, in the town of Woodboro, that Dan had disappeared. He had begged to take the horses there because he was proud of them. A Plain Man could be proud of horses even if he was not supposed to be proud of himself.

Father had agreed to let Dan go. He even helped to prepare the horses and drive them into town. But afterward their nearest neighbor, John, brought the horses home.

"Your son Daniel has told me to bring the horses," John said. Esther would never forget how he looked when he said it, with his blood gone from his face. He did not look at Father as he spoke, but first at the ground and then at the sky.

"Where is Daniel then?" Father asked.

John said only, "He sent this letter."

It was terrible to remember how Father looked when he read Dan's letter. He stood reading it in the dooryard, the wind blowing around him, lifting his hair and his beard. While he stood reading, John turned and went away, out of the place and down the road.

Father stood in the yard for a long time, holding the letter in his hand, at his side. Mother went to him. Esther could not hear what they said to each other, and was afraid to go closer to listen. When Father came into the house at last, he had the look he brought into church with him on a special day. He walked to the stove, walking so slowly that Esther knew when each foot came down, one after the other.

When the stove lid was lifted, fire shone upward onto Father's curling beard. He put the letter into the flames and stood still until it was entirely burned. Then he took the poker and stirred angrily until even the shape of the letter had vanished among the coals.

It was then he said, "We will not speak of Daniel here again."

Downstairs, Esther heard a young man's light laugh. But it was Hans, not Dan. Had Hans ever wondered about whether buttons could harm a man's soul? No, it was impossible to think such a thing of Hans.

Father and Mother were getting up. What a fine big breakfast there would be this morning, to celebrate! Esther jumped up and began to dress, not to miss a thing. She almost forgot to say her morning prayer, but not quite, for this one was always about Dan.

"Help Dan to come back home. Help everything here to be the way it was before." But this time she added something else, for herself, thinking of the school and hearing the happy laughter of the lovers in the kitchen when Mother discovered them: *"And help me never to take The First Step Away!"*

4

THE GIRL IN PINK

Ruth would be married the first Tuesday in November. Even before school started, a week after Hans' light had come into the window, the house was humming with work and plans. Esther was so busy and excited she almost forgot about school. But, of course, never entirely. In the middle of gathering eggs or putting away dishes or peeling potatoes, she would suddenly think: *"Next week I am going to school!"*

What a mixup her feelings were! She was glad and she was curious. But she was worried too. From going to town and even to the Fair, she knew how it was going to be in many ways. She could not show more if she wore a dress the color of a cardinal. Only in a crowd of dark dresses exactly alike, and white bonnets and black shoes and white aprons, was she hidden. At the Fair, where hundreds of people wore different styles and colors, she had been absolutely clear and alone among them, like one black bird against the sky. At school she would show every day, every hour.

At the Fair, in a little booth, there had been a wooden bird held up for men to shoot with guns. She would be held up like that, alone, at school.

The time came closer and closer. Friday. Saturday. Sunday. It was not until they had come home from meeting Sunday night that Father mentioned what was going to happen the next morning.

Mother said, as usual, "Esther, it is time for bed."

Father reached out and touched her as she passed him, and said, "Sit down at the table for a little. There is something we must talk about. Besides—" he looked at Mother and nodded toward the cupboard where the books were kept. "If you will bring the Book, I have something to read."

Esther sat down. Ruth sat down too, with her knitting. Mother brought the Bible and set it in front of Father, sitting down beside him, then, with her hands folded on her lap.

"Tomorrow, Esther, you must begin at the school," Father said.

Esther's fingers wanted to move on her lap, but she held them quiet. Only her toes stirred in her high shoes, wiggling and wiggling.

"Later we will try to have a school of our own here," he said, "but now they say you must go to this one for a while." He looked steadily at her. "The children at this school are different."

She looked down at her quiet fingers.

"You will see many different things," Father said. He glanced at Mother and seemed to wait for her to add something.

So she said, "Esther has seen some of those different things already. On the streets and in the town."

"But not in the same room!" Father said. And he turned to the worn big book before him. He knew this book so well that it did not take him long to find what he wanted, and Esther knew from what he chose to read that he too had been thinking of The First Step Away.

" 'Behold,' " he read, " 'we put bits in the horses' mouths, that they may obey us; and we turn about their whole body.' You see the meaning of this, Esther? A small thing may seem smaller than it really is."

This was true. Mother sat nodding.

" 'Behold also the ships, which though they be so great, and are driven of fierce winds, yet are they turned about with a very small helm . . .' "

She had never seen a ship, but she had heard of them. Mother had seen ships near Philadelphia; she often told of them with wonder.

" 'Even so, the tongue is a little member, and

boasteth great things. Behold, how great a matter a little fire kindleth!' " He looked closely at her. "Esther, I only tell you these things so you will understand why it is you will remain by yourself. Though we have learned always to love our enemies, and so never fight . . ."

Ruth gave a little gasp at his words and he looked at her. She blushed and said nothing, though he was looking a question. Mother said quickly, "Ruth means the children in the school are not enemies."

"I did not finish," Father said. "I meant only to say they were not her friends. Esther will look at the teacher and do as the teacher says, unless it is something she is told never to do, here at home. But I do not expect her to look at the children."

Ruth looked closely at her knitting and pretended to count. Mother said anxiously, "Except—"

"Except to keep from falling over them!" Father said, and smiled. Mother smiled too, then, and Ruth.

Esther was glad they smiled.

"Now," Father said in a gentle voice, "you may go to bed."

Esther wanted to tell Father what she had been thinking lately, and that she would never, never go away. But she could not find the words to say it with. Even the next morning when only the two of them rode in the wagon, out of the yard and down the road toward the school, she could find no words. One reason she could not say it, of course, was that she could think of no way to do so without mentioning the name of Dan. Even if school had been Away for Dan, it need not be Away for her. What Father had read was good to remember. If you did not kindle a little fire in the first place, you would never have a big one that you could not manage to put out.

The bell rang as they turned the last great bend in the road and saw the school on its little hill. Esther jumped, and Father said, "It is only the first bell. There are always two, one five minutes early so slow scholars will hurry."

She had known this, for Dan had told her. She had jumped because of the exciting thought that the bell was ringing now for *her*. But she did not say so.

Father helped her down outside the school. He handed her the lunch-basket and said, "I will be here waiting for you when school is over at three o'clock."

Suddenly she realized how many hours it was going to be. She turned to say this to him, but he drove away without looking back, and she was alone.

She stood still. For the life of her she could not stir off the road and over the bridge and onto the school-

lot where children were running in every direction.
Nobody seemed to notice her at all.

Then the bell rang again. A woman appeared in the
doorway at the top of two wide stone steps. She called
something and the children began to run toward her.
When they stood in a long crooked line, one behind
the other, she stood aside and they marched in.

Esther looked down the road where Father had disappeared. But then she heard the teacher calling from the door again. "Hello! Aren't you coming in?"

Esther had to move now, she knew it. She took a deep trembling breath and crossed the bridge. She did not look up at all, but only at the path and at the steps and then at the teacher's white shoes fastened with a neat row of buttons on either foot.

"Your name is Esther Lapp?" the teacher asked.

Esther nodded.

"We are glad to see you," the teacher said, and took

Esther's hand. Inside she led the way down an aisle between two long rows of seats. What a noise! Everywhere were laughing and whispering, like a thousand starlings in a tree.

"You will sit here," the teacher said, and Esther felt the good strong seat under her. She sat looking at the desk. The wooden top was covered with scribbles she could not read very well and with pictures of things she did not recognize. The teacher went to the front of the room and rapped with a little stick and the noise gradually died away.

Things began to move by. Hands went up. The teacher talked and called out one name and another. Pencils were passed in long boxes. Paper came in sheets, some colored, just as Dan had said. There was a small pair of scissors and a large box of crayons. And then there were books, lovely, lovely books with pictures of more things than Esther had ever seen. Looking at the pictures she did not have to look at the children, and presently she began to breathe deeply again.

At noon she sat still when the others went outside. Her lunch-basket lay under her desk, but she did not feel at all hungry. The teacher came to her and said in a kind voice, "Would you rather eat here today? Don't you want to go outside in the sun?"

She shook her head.

The teacher went back to her own big desk and ate a lunch from a paper bag. She had a long blue container, too, that had milk in it, and a small red cup for a cap. She did not say anything, but when she saw Esther eating slowly and looking at the cup, she smiled. Presently she went again to ring the bell.

The very first person to come in was a girl dressed all in pink. When she appeared, Esther was looking at the door, but dropped her eyes so quickly she saw only a kind of pink cloud, really, like the heart of a sunset.

The pink cloud came down the aisle and stopped beside the desk in front of Esther's. Now Esther remembered seeing the pink dress before, over her book.

"Hello," said the pink cloud, and Esther looked up. "Are you Amish?"

Esther nodded. The girl sat down but twisted herself about in the seat and smiled. "I'm *glad* I sit by you," she said.

Suddenly, though she did not know why the girl was glad, Esther felt glad too. She did not say so, but only sat looking at her desk and then, once more, at the wonderful books. The children all came in, filling the room with noise and motion, until the teacher rapped, again, with her stick.

It was still very bad, for Esther felt squeezed into her

desk and into the room and into the crowd of children and even her heart felt tight and her stomach a little sick. But it was not as bad as it had been that morning. Over her book, over her pencil and paper, somehow between Esther and all of the others, was the girl in pink. Twice during the afternoon she turned with a smile.

Never in her life had Esther dreamed how wonderful it could be to see Father sitting in the buggy, after school finally ended, waiting for her to come. He sat very straight, looking neither to the right or to the left, even when the teacher called, "Good afternoon!"

As they drove off down the road toward home, Esther looked back once and saw the girl in pink lift her hand to wave good-by. But of course she did not lift her hand to answer, or even so much as glance back again. Father did not mention the school. He did not even ask her how the day had been, but began to tell her of all the things that had happened at home during the day.

5

THE FIRST STEP AWAY

For days the school made Esther feel so tight and so terrible that she could scarcely wait until it ended and she could hurry outside where Father sat patiently in the buggy, waiting behind the patient horses, whose names she knew. Each day she could not wait to pat them and speak to them.

The teacher was kind enough. She wore colored shirts and was pleasant to look at when she sat still at her desk. But when she got up she was entirely too thin. Her bones looked uncomfortable, showing at the base of her neck and in hard wing-points, like the wings of a plucked chicken, when she wrote on the blackboard. Her voice stretched and broke in two when the boys made her cross. For a few days they did it on purpose, many many times. Esther felt ashamed for them and looked at the floor when it happened. But the boys did not seem in the least ashamed.

Esther did as Father had told her and never looked at the children—at least when they were looking at her. But almost every time she glanced up, somebody was looking. They laughed too. Jumpy laughter. All of a sudden one of them would burst out and then everybody else joined in. It made Esther want to laugh too, so her throat ached with laughter. But then she learned that the laughter was unkind.

She knew this because the teacher scolded about it.

"Now we *won't* have this silly laughing!" she said, and pounded on the desk with her little stick.

But they did have it, anyhow, whether she said *Yes* or *No,* and no matter how hard she pounded.

Esther didn't know the laughing was at *her* until the girl in pink said it. She was sitting directly in front of Esther, and did not laugh. Instead, she turned around suddenly one day and said, *"I'm* not laughing at you! I wouldn't!"

Esther looked at her in surprise. Of course it was good to know she *wouldn't,* but it was not good to know the others *were.* She felt her face begin to burn.

"I like you!" said the girl in pink. "My name is Mary."

Mary was the most beautiful and important name in the world for a girl. Esther had always thought so. This Mary, her skin as rosy as her dress, had hair that fell in little golden curls like wisps of silk. Sometimes a curl almost went into Esther's ink-bottle. It never quite went in, but brushed over. Esther reached out once and moved the curl away. It was exactly like the silk in a milkweed pod. It felt like a downy feather. It was so beautiful it made a shiver go through her fingers, and her heart suddenly beat very fast.

Father would not like her to be friends with Mary, or even to look at her. If anybody in the world was really different from Esther herself and all her people, that one was Mary. She wore pink one day and blue the next and then yellow, but Esther liked pink the best. She laughed a good deal. She tossed her hair when the boys chased her in the games at recess, and squealed when they caught her. All the other girls wanted to walk by her side and whisper with her, back and forth. Even when she did not wear the pink dress, Esther still thought of her as The Pink Girl. This was because of her pretty skin and her hands, on which she wore two small rings. Then her knees were pink and her plump legs, which were bare from her little socks upward until they vanished in her fluffy skirt. Mary was like the pretty girls made of glass in shop windows.

"How beautiful you are!" Esther thought many times a day.

One morning Mary turned around with a smile

during the writing exercise. "I'm writing you a letter," she said. "Why don't you write one to me?"

Esther looked at the pencil in her hand. She had been making great A's and B's and C's and all the other letters in perfect rows. She knew how to put some of them together; she could make a great many words. But she knew she should not think about writing a letter to Mary. Father had said, "You will not look at the other children," and already she looked at Mary all the time, as much as possible. Writing a letter would be worse than looking, she knew that without being told. She went on making A's and B's and C's in perfect rows.

Soon Mary turned around again. She slipped a folded paper onto Esther's desk.

"Haven't you written mine yet?" she whispered.

Esther's mouth felt dry and she swallowed deeply before she could answer. "Not yet," she said.

It was like a promise. She had not meant it to be, but it was. Mary smiled and said, "It gets easier and easier to write. You'll learn soon. Letters are good practice." She turned back to her desk.

The folded note lay on Esther's desk. She looked at it for a long time before she touched it. Was receiving a letter as bad as writing one? Father received letters from seed companies and from the school officials and

many others who lived outside the neighborhood. After all, if somebody sent you a letter, it wasn't your fault, was it? She thought of Dan here in the school-room year after year. Did somebody in pink send let-ters to Dan? Or maybe somebody with buttons on his coat? All the boys had buttons on their coats.

She picked up the letter and unfolded it. In very tall wriggly letters, Mary had written:

Dear Friend Esther:

I like you. I think your dress is pretty. Your apron is cute too. And your little hat.

Your friend,

Mary.

She sat still. What a kind good letter it was! How could Mary think such a dark dress was pretty? The white apron was very common and plain, yet Mary thought it was cute. A nice little word—cute! cute! cute! It was like a canary singing. She lifted her hand to her bonnet, tied securely under her chin with her hair tucked under. It was possible that her own hair would make curls, she thought. When she took out the braids and combed it at night, it fell in wide waves over her shoulders.

Even the Bible said, "If a woman have long hair, it is a glory to her. . . ."

Suddenly she felt happy, the way she sometimes felt when she woke and the sun was shining in her window. Mary turned to see whether the letter had been opened, and smiled.

Esther must say something, she knew. Not to say something would be unkind, and she was taught always to return one kindness with another. Or perhaps even with two. "Thank you very much," she said. "It is a beautiful letter."

"As soon as you can, write one to me," Mary said. Then, "Do you play jump-the-rope? Would you like to jump with me at recess?"

Esther caught her breath. She had watched the girls jumping every day but never even thought of jumping herself. "I don't know how," she said.

Mary looked surprised. "It's easy," she said. "I'll teach you. Except—maybe—do you think your skirt will get in the way?"

The teacher rapped sharply with her little stick. "No whispering!" she said. "Mary, have you finished the exercise?"

"No, ma'am," Mary said.

"Then work, don't visit," the teacher said. "It's almost time for recess."

Mary gave a quick little glance at Esther, and winked an eye! She had not finished her exercise because she had written a letter. It was their secret. She began to write very fast on the exercise. Esther could watch the motion of her pretty pink elbow as she wrote.

Esther tucked the letter inside her desk. She could look at it every day at school, she thought. Every day she could know again that Mary thought her dress was pretty, that her apron was cute, and so was her little hat. "I wish I could show Mary my long hair!" she thought.

Suddenly, then, she thought about Vanity. Hair was tucked away under bonnets so there would be no thinking about brushing and curling. A cold wind seemed to blow through her very soul. Could Mary's letter—such a kind thing!—be The First Step Away? It was impossible. . . .

The bell rang. Instantly, like a sudden burst of water, the children began to flow out of the room.

"Don't push," the teacher said. "In order now! The third grade is first out today. Harry—take your turn. Kenneth—"

Mary rose in front of Esther and they waited for their turn to march. In the most natural way in the world, Mary took Esther's hand in her own. Her hand was soft and warm, as kind as her letter. Esther felt the turn of her fingers. "*I* know!" Mary said. "We'll play jacks instead of jump-the-rope. Just you and I. We don't *want* to jump!"

"I've never played jacks either," Esther said.

"You haven't? Well, I'll show you. It's as easy as fun," Mary said.

Always, her whole life, Esther had learned what kindness was. It was to think of others before yourself. It was to think of their comfort before your own. This Mary had thought of how hard it would be to jump in a long dress with high shoes and heavy stockings. A long skirt would switch and catch in the rope. But jacks—Esther had never played, but she had watched the others play at recess several times. It was simple, bouncing a little ball and picking up first one jack, then two, until you swept up all eight at the same time.

Mary kept her hand. "We speak for the step!" she cried the minute they were outside. "Esther and I get the step!"

The others looked at them in surprise, the two of them together.

"You jump," Mary said to the girls who usually played with her. "I've promised to show Esther how to play jacks. Then we'll all have a game."

So she managed to get them out of the way. They wouldn't be standing around watching while Esther was clumsy, as she was learning. The step was sunny and warm and the maples around the schoolyard were changing color. The air was all golden because of the leaves. Tossing the ball and picking up the clever little jackstones was a beautiful thing to be doing. One—two—three! She felt them sweep into her hand together.

"Good! Good!" Mary said.

When the bell rang she said, "Next time you'll be able to get them all."

Oh, it was lovely to march beside Mary, proudly into the school again. Nobody laughed. It was as if Esther was just like all the rest.

Sometimes Father was so busy that he came later than the school bus. Esther had never wondered why she shouldn't go in the bus with the others and save her father the trouble of leaving his work to come for her. She knew the reason: Plain People did not ride in machines. That day it seemed foolish to her for the first time. She remembered Dan coming along the road in the car with the boys. "I always wondered . . ." he had said. "Now I know."

Mary waved to her from the window of the bus. "See you Monday, Esther!" she called. "See you Monday!" For it was Friday today.

Esther had always been glad when it was Friday

before. Now she was sorry. There was all that quiet sitting in church between Friday and Monday. No pink girl would be sitting in front of her, but only children in black and gray and purple and dark brown. Her own Sunday dress was the color of dead leaves that had lain under snow all winter long.

She sat on the step to wait, exactly where she had sat at recess a while before. The leaves glowed brighter as the sun lowered. And there seemed to be another glow besides, where Mary had sat bouncing the ball. Being kind. There were kind good people, then, who wore pink. And blue. And red. All colors . . .

She stood up as she heard the buggy coming. Her heart beat fast as if she had been discovered at a mischief. Or with something she had stolen and must hide away.

⌒ 6 ⌒

SWEET WATER—AND BITTER

This Sunday the meeting was to be held at Esther's own house. On Saturday it was necessary to go into the town for supplies for the dinner. Mother always walked just behind Father, who bought everything. Esther always walked just behind Mother and helped carry the bundles.

Walking past the shop windows toward the grocery store, Esther noticed something in the Five-and-Ten. There were always hundreds of interesting little things in those windows. She had stood looking with Dan several times when Father was busy. But today she saw something special, so special that she forgot to go on walking behind Mother. Besides many other things, there were piles of jackstones in the window, exactly like Mary's. Esther could not have counted how many there were if she had stood by the window all day. Some were the color of new pennies. But some were red and some were green. There were also piles of bright red rubber balls to do the bouncing.

"If only I could have some of my own!" she thought. Only eight out of all those hundreds, that was all she needed. And one little ball. Then she could practice bouncing and picking up. Soon she might learn to do harder things, like "eggs in the basket."

Suddenly, behind her, Father spoke. She had been so interested in the window she hadn't heard him come back where she stood. He said, "Cheap! Cheap!" like an angry sparrow.

As they walked on again, he kept her carefully beside him on the street. And on the way home, after the groceries were bought and piled in the back of the buggy, he suddenly burst out, "Trash!" His voice was like the falling of a tree.

There was a great deal to do for the Meeting, even though many came in to help. The front of the house was made with partitions which could be opened so the rooms ran together. Furniture was taken out and benches set in rows. Dinner was cooked for everybody, besides little pies for the children to eat during the long speaking.

It wasn't hard for Esther to sit still to the end of the speaking. To sit still was one of the first things she ever learned. It was strange to her, at school, how the rows of children wiggled and shook and reached

and stuck their feet out and in. The teacher often said, "For goodness' sakes, don't you know how to sit still?"

Of course she never said it to Esther. Esther could sit in her chair exactly like a stone. She had learned how to do that before she even knew she was a girl. Before she knew she was Esther, a person of her own. She had never thought about *how* to sit still. It was maybe like being a frog on a green rock; she was part of the stillness. Or a woodcock on a nest in the grass. In a way, you simply pretended you were not there at all.

She was proud that she could keep her motions inside herself entirely, like a frog. She had watched one closely down by the watering pond, and saw his stretched skin move in and out with his heart's beating. She liked hearing her own noises and feeling her own moving. Breathing in and out. Heart swinging to and fro. Or sometimes her stomach growling like an ogre under a bridge. It could happen, when there had been too much cabbage for supper on Saturday, that the ogre was too loud entirely in the middle of a meeting. Then people smiled and looked at their laps. But sometimes they had ogres too, which was why they smiled and understood.

After singing, her father, who was one of the two Denier Zum Buch, a preacher, made the beginning. This speaking took half an hour, ending with a prayer and a reading from the Bible. Then the chief sermon, which must be nearly two hours long to be considered of any use to anybody. During this time the pies would be passed to the children. Then more singing and the men rose and went out. Then the young women went out, then the older ones, then all the rest. The benches were moved again and tables set up for dinner, one table for men and one for women. After that the men would talk about crops and news of Plain People who lived in other places, while the women washed dishes.

It was all pleasant, even when the speaking was long, for one could think one's own thoughts without interruption. Today Esther thought, "Tomorrow it is Monday again. Mary and I will sit practicing on the steps. Imagine, to have a whole set of jackstones, to carry them home in a little bag at night! Bounce the ball to a count of three, *one* toss it up, *two* bounce it while you gather up the jackstones quick, quick, *three* catch it in your hand again. A *little* toss or you lose track of the ball while you find the jackstone. Then you've missed."

She noticed Mother's eyes on her. Her hands had been making little motions in her lap. She wound her fingers tight together and sat still, pretending she wasn't there for a while. But soon the bouncing began again in her mind. One—two—three!

I have my savings in the little box Dan carved for me, she thought. If only I could get into that store for a minute by myself! But she knew this was impossible. Perhaps Mary would get them for her . . . "Mary, if you go where the jacks are, I would like two green, two copper, two red, two silver, and a little ball."

"Why, of course!" Mary said in Esther's mind, looking very pink.

It would be hard to carry jackstones and a ball around without them being seen. Mary's letter she had slipped inside her stocking, over her knee; even a thing so small kept creeping down until it made a queer square lump over the top of her shoe. Maybe jackstones and a ball could be tied into a knot at the edge of her petticoat. But *tight,* so they'd never rattle . . . She would feel them bounce as she walked.

The preacher had finished speaking and turned to his Bible. "I will read from *James,*" he said, and he began. It was the same as the reading Father gave the night before school began! About the horses and the ships.

Esther felt her heart beating too loud altogether. When she looked down she could see it pushing at her dress just the way the frog's heart pushed at his skin. It was for *her* the preacher was reading. What had made her think she could hide her thoughts here at the Meeting itself, where the People read and sang and prayed? She had sat all that time without even listening to what was said, but now the words, read slowly and strongly, came to her one by one like the striking of a clock. Jackstones were very small, small enough to hide in a knot of her petticoat. But hiding them away—that was as huge as any lie.

The preacher read more than Father read that

morning. After the words, *How great a matter a little
fire kindleth!* he read about a fountain. *Doth a fountain send forth at the same time sweet water and
bitter?*

Esther had heard the meaning of that plenty of
times: *A person cannot be bad and good at the same
time.* She held her fingers tighter than ever in her lap.
Her heart beat louder and pushed harder at her dress.
Would Mother notice? She lifted her hands to cover
the place where her heart was beating.

Tomorrow she would tell Mary she could not play
jacks any more.

The thought filled her with bitter sorrow at the
same time she was glad to be strong. Perhaps one could
not be bad and good at once, but one could be both
glad and sorry. Glad to be doing right. But sorry to
say, "I can't be your friend."

A new speaker began. Soon Mother beckoned. It
was time to pass out the little pies, for children were
becoming restless. As usual, fathers were folding their
handkerchiefs into white mice with pointed ears, and
into twins-in-a-cradle, to entertain the children on
their knees. Esther saw several of them look relieved
when they saw Mother moving toward the kitchen
with Ruth following close behind.

Esther was proud to help with such things.

After Meeting had ended at last, some of the other girls helped with the table and the food. Sarah was always one of the busiest.

"How is school, Esther?" she asked as they carried plates to the table. "Do you like it?"

Esther swallowed hard, thinking of Mary. Then she said, "No. Not very much!"

"Well," Sarah said, surprised. "I hoped you might. I liked it when I had been there for a little while. Of course, others were going at the same time when I was there. I remember how much D—" She stopped. But Esther knew what she had meant to say if she had not noticed Mother coming. She had meant to say that she remembered how much Dan liked the school.

People were laughing and talking to Ruth as she moved among them, lightly and happily as if she now owned the world. "It is only a little while now," they said. "Will your wedding dress be blue or gray?"

"Blue," Ruth answered. She asked all of the women to come to a quilting the first Saturday in October.

A quilting! Esther felt a little better. Even if she could never play jacks, she would always be able to go to a quilting.

7

ESTHER ASKS A QUESTION

Never in all her life had Esther dreaded anything so much as telling Mary she could not play again. Father left her at the schoolhouse early, before even the teacher came, for he had work to do. Father was always on time for everything, or else ahead of time. He knew a saying, "One who wastes Time wastes Life itself."

Esther sat alone on the very step where she and Mary could no longer play. The sky was full of plunging gray clouds. Maybe it would rain. Maybe nobody would be able to go outside today. Then she could wait and tell Mary tomorrow.

The school bus was coming. It was bright orange, very beautiful on the brown road between the green and yellow trees. It was pleasant to watch the big door swing open and the children come out one by one. They looked gay. Every one had a different color; you couldn't know which color would come out next. One was blue and one was red. A yellow sweater. Then a green cap! One boy had no cap, but his hair was exactly the color of a robin's breast. If she had *that,* Esther thought, how cheerful it would be, better than if she could have a bright scarf and mittens—for nobody could object to colored hair. Objecting to a bright beautiful color that grew out of you and belonged to you would be foolish. It would be as foolish as objecting to colored flowers, or carrots. Or cardinals. Or beetles. Or berries. Or to sunshine itself.

Mary came out of the bus. At the same moment the sun came out of the clouds, and Mary was shining as she ran. "Esther, if it rains she lets us play jacks on the floor!" she said. She had been thinking about it too. Esther felt a sudden wave of happiness. Mary had been thinking about playing again, just as she had herself. As naturally as could be, Mary took hold of her hand and they went into the schoolhouse together. It did not even occur to Esther to tell Mary that she couldn't play. After all, there was plenty of time.

In writing class, Mary turned and slipped another note onto Esther's desk. She did it so quickly that Esther hardly saw the motion. But there was the note, neatly folded, with *Esther* printed on it in letters nearly an inch high.

What would it say this time? She had started to

unfold it before she remembered about the preaching the day before and how strong she had meant to be. Her fingers trembled. *But Mary was sweet,* she thought. Nobody could deny it who saw her at her desk with her head lowered over her work, clean and neat and pretty with her hair shining and tied with a pink ribbon. Like the fountain, Mary could not possibly be bitter too. Maybe that was what the Bible meant!

Of course. Why hadn't she thought of it before? Firmly, she unfolded Mary's note.

> Dear Friend Esther:
> Why don't you write a letter to me?
>> Your friend,
>> Mary.

Esther sat as still as she had ever sat in church. Why didn't she? She had learned from the beginning that when one received a kindness, a kindness should be given in return as soon as possible. Mother said that all the time, and Father too.

Well, then— She tore a sheet of paper from her notebook and began to make letters carefully. They didn't look as good as Mary's, no matter how carefully she made them. She reached into her desk and brought out Mary's first note. Then she began on a fresh sheet:

Dear Friend Mary:

I like you too. I think your pink dress is pretty. And your hair is cute. Your friend,

Esther.

She folded it very small and neat. Then she had an idea. She reached down and pulled a dark purple thread out of her dress. She was glad her dress was purple today and not black. With the thread she tied a neat little bow, so the letter looked like a package. She dropped it over Mary's shoulder, onto her desk. Her heart was beating hard as it had in the Meeting; she felt it thumping against the desk as she leaned forward. Now it was done, she thought.

Mary turned with a quick smile. She liked the package with its little bow. And then Esther watched as she opened it, hardly breathing. What would she say? But writing class ended before anything could be said. It was time for recess, and the sun had decided to shine, after all.

How could she say, "I can't play with you again." It was not possible. Mary took her hand as the line moved forward. Esther could not have taken away her hand any more than she could draw a sword from a stone. In two minutes they were on the step, bouncing the ball, gathering up the jacks, bouncing and gathering. "Good! Good!" Mary said whenever Esther did not miss. When the ball dropped or rolled away or when one of the jacks escaped, Mary never squealed with pleasure the way most of the girls always did. Instead, she would say, "Too bad! They were scattered too far that time." Or even, "The ball went crooked; it bounced on that crack in the step."

All afternoon Esther felt happy and light-hearted and gay. She ate her lunch in a huge circle of girls, under a tree. Nobody laughed in an unkind way. She did not look down all the time, but up and around to see what everybody was doing.

As the children went out to the orange bus again, Esther saw Father coming far down the road. Mary stopped beside her, by the step. "See you tomorrow!" she said.

Would Father notice? No, Esther thought, relieved, he was still too far away.

"Good-by," she said quickly, and sat down on the step.

But Mary did not go just then. The children were filing onto the bus. She had plenty of time. "Once I was in a play," Mary said, and sat down on the step too. "I took the part of a Pilgrim—it was a Thanksgiving play—and I had a dress just like yours."

"A dress like *mine?*" It seemed strange to think of Mary in such a dress.

"I love wearing long dresses," Mary said. "And those darling little high shoes—with laces. And bonnets that tie under the chin."

Father was coming very close now.

"You'll miss getting on the bus," Esther said.

Mary stood up. "If you'd like," she said quickly, "some day at recess—when I wear my pink—we can go out to the girls' place and *change.* Just for the rest of the day."

She didn't wait for an answer, but had to run. Somebody was calling her. It was lucky she hadn't waited, either, because Esther was completely without words to say. *Change?* She looked down at her dress and the tips of her black shoes. She hardly saw or heard the bus go roaring away. When she looked up again, Father was driving out of the cloud of dust it left behind it, looking very angry. She saw him glance back at the roaring thing that made such an ugliness out of a good road.

At first Esther did not speak, beyond her greeting. She was thinking about what Mary had said. If only she could tell Father and he would understand!

"And how is it going at school?" he asked kindly, at last.

"Very well."

"Do you read in the books yet?"

"Mostly in one book."

"And you write the letters?"

Her heart bounced like the little red ball. How did he *know?* But then she realized what it was he meant. He did not mean letters to Mary, but the letters A and B and C and all the rest.

"Yes," she said, relieved. "All of the alphabet now."

He drove along in silence awhile. The horse went clip-clop-clop, clip-clop-clop, a sound Esther loved.

"It's too bad you are the only one of the Plain children at the school just now," Father said. "It isn't easy to be alone there. But next year there will be the Yoder child, and the year after, several others."

She looked up at him gratefully. Perhaps he did know, after all, exactly how hard it was. He had said, *"It isn't* easy . . ." She thought, "I'll ask him. It'll be all right to ask him now." But she didn't know exactly what to ask, or how. She swallowed twice and then began slowly, looking straight ahead down the road. "I've been wondering since I came to school—"

He did not look at her either. He gazed at the rump of the horse going from side to side. "Yes, Esther?" he asked.

"I've been wondering why— Well—" Her voice

stopped as on the edge of a cold pool and then plunged: "Why is it that people must wear different clothes?" She would like it if she had been able to ask the question the way Dan did, how buttons might harm a man's soul. But this was good enough to begin with. She knew her question was well understood.

"You have been wondering why *we* wear different clothes, Esther?" he asked.

"Yes," she said.

He did not answer until he had turned the buggy into their own farm and the horse had stopped by the barn. He did not offer to get out of the buggy, but sat still for a while. Esther sat still beside him, looking at the horse and at her hands in her lap and at the toes of her shoes.

"It is not only *wearing*," he said at last. "It is *who we are*. It is what we believe." He said it with his strongest look; she knew the look was there even before she raised her eyes to his face. It was the look he had when he swung an ax over his head, or when he carried a big stone. It was stronger than the look he read the Bible with.

"We are Plain People," he said, "and so we wear plain clothes. There are not very many in the world now who live as it was intended in the beginning."

She knew he believed every word and was proud because he believed them.

"But why—" She paused, to be sure of what she meant to say. She looked up, puzzled, to ask it, with Mary in her thoughts. "Who are *they*, then? The others? They wear different clothes nearly every day." Inside herself she was asking, "Who is Mary?"

His voice was still strong, but heavy too, like something boiled too thick. "They don't know who they are!" he said. "They are something different every day! They are anything and everything, those people. They are like beans in a hat. They are nothing and nobody!"

Now he seemed very angry and it was almost as if she had shouted "Daniel! Daniel! Who is Daniel?" Or even "Who is Dan?" He got down and began to unharness the horse with impatient hands. Esther saw Mother coming from the house to welcome her.

All evening she thought about what Father had said. It sounded sensible and true. Each living thing had its special color, and this never varied among its kind except sometimes for the seasons. You were Red Squirrel, or you were Gray Squirrel. If Red you were quarrelsome and your meat was not sweet and good and you drove Gray out of the trees and robbed him of his nuts. If you were a mouse instead you had another gray, smooth and flat, and a different tail without fuzz on it. If you were a woodcock you had still another gray, but had a bill for bug-digging added onto the front of you and eyes that never blinked for fear of missing something important. Or dangerous.

Every one "after its own kind" as the Bible said God made them right at first.

But when she thought once more about herself, something was wrong again. Something was different with all those creatures and with people. Not until the middle of the night did she see what the difference was. She woke suddenly with it quite clear in her mind. People were not different, like squirrels and mice and woodcocks. Underneath their clothes they were all the same. She blushed to be thinking about such a thing, but it was true. So the difference was that *people made who they were with their wearing.* For people, wearing this and that didn't come naturally at all, like fur and pinfeathers. They decided for themselves who they would be. Even Adam and Eve had decided, had they not?

Father and Mother had decided. That was what he had meant. Plain People, with nothing fancy or bright to distract them. Dan had not made up his mind to be Plain, and when they tried to make it up for him, he went away.

And she herself. She must decide too. Sometime, not very long away, she must decide. Her mind swung to and fro, to and fro. Here were Father and Mother and so many good kind ones who cared about everything she thought and did. But here was Mary, smiling on the other side. And curiously enough, beside Mary stood Dan, tall and handsome as she remembered him.

She sat straight up in bed. Had Dan fallen in love, then? With somebody away, not Sarah? With somebody he could walk with in the town, and speak with even before he turned his light into her window? The thought made such a great shivering that she drew the covers tight under her chin. *With somebody in a pink dress?*

Now she recalled the row of small pink buttons down the back of Mary's dress.

If only she could see Dan now! Dan is the one to tell, she thought. I could ask Dan every question and he would answer. She was filled with loneliness for him. How far away had he gone? If she searched and asked questions, could she find him? He had not taken his buggy or his horse, so he could not have gone very far.

Shivering, she slipped out of bed and said her prayers all over again, from the beginning. But one prayer was different now. Usually she said, "Help Dan to be all right wherever he is, and help him to come home." Now she said, "Help me to find Dan. Help me to see him soon."

Back under the covers, she went instantly to sleep. Whenever she made a good prayer she felt peaceful afterward. Every prayer she had ever made for a good and necessary thing had always been answered. In her sleep she did not even stir or dream.

8

SARAH AND THE BRIGHT NEWS

In spite of being so sure about the prayer, Esther was surprised when the answer began to happen right away. It began that very Saturday, at the quilting.

Every Amish woman for miles around came to help stitch Ruth's quilt. Mother and Ruth had put up the quilting frames in the parlor, stretching the cloth and the padding upon it. A circle of chairs were set all the way around. For days and days Ruth had cut out bright designs from an old pattern that had been made by her great-great-grandmother, or perhaps, Mother said, by a grandmother even greater.

The women sat around the huge quilt and stitched and stitched, contesting with each other for the neatest, shortest stitches. To make them short and neat was not easy, for each one must go through design and cloth and padding, clear to the other side. As they worked the quilt would be rolled inward from the edges, the circle of chairs getting smaller and smaller.

It was a cheerful design, yellow and red and blue

birds perched upon brown twigs among bright green leaves and gaily colored flowers. "Oh, how pretty it is!" Esther cried, as she saw the design growing.

"You have one like this on your own bed," said Mother. "Every woman in my family has a quilt with this same design."

Esther could not believe it until she went upstairs to look. Yes, the design was the same, but the birds were almost faded away. Much washing in strong soap and drying in bright sun had by now faded the poor things almost out of sight.

"Mine has the same birds, but they are dull," she said when she came back down.

How they laughed! Women at a quilting seemed to laugh at every little thing. Rebecca, the oldest woman there and Hans' grandmother, looked at Ruth and said, "You see, Ruth, everything will grow dull in time."

"But not Hans!" Ruth cried, to please them, and again laughter filled the room.

Everybody began teasing, and they laughed and talked and sang and stitched, hour after hour. Even Sarah laughed and once she said to Ruth, "Who do you suppose will be the next bride after you?"

Why did she say it? Ruth blushed and the women

looked at each other. All the laughter stopped suddenly and Mother went to the kitchen quickly. Why had Sarah said such a thing, when everybody knew she had been in love with Dan, who had gone away? For a minute Esther thought the party was spoiled. But it was not. Sarah mentioned several names of girls her own age, teasing them about this boy and that boy who took them home from church and from the sings. She was so good-natured that everybody became cheerful again right away. Her cheeks were pink and her eyes looked glad.

So, Esther thought, Sarah has stopped feeling sad about Dan. Perhaps she was even in love with somebody else; how could that ever be? Perhaps it was wise for her to forget Dan, but it made Esther sad all the same to think of it. Sarah behaved today as if she hadn't a care in the world. She was the prettiest girl Esther had ever seen, with sleek shining hair disappearing into a cap that was as white as snow. Her cheeks and lips were very red and her eyes were large and full of twinkling. What a shame Dan had not loved Sarah enough, Esther thought for the thousandth time.

When the quilt was rolled almost halfway in, she found out something about Sarah. She should have known by the laughing and talking and the bright eyes.

For what girl who had loved Dan could ever love anybody else?

It was part of her work to help Ruth to press the bits of bright cloth for the design, carrying them from the kitchen to be laid in place for stitching. She was giving one to Sarah, when Sarah leaned close to her ear and whispered, "I have something to tell you."

She looked full into Sarah's eyes for only a second and knew it was about Dan. Sarah gave a little nod, and suddenly Esther's hands began to tremble. She was afraid all the women would notice how clumsy she was.

"I would like a drink of water, Esther. I am thirsty," Sarah said. She stood up, pushing her chair away from the frame.

"Never mind getting up. Esther will be glad to bring it," Mother said.

But Sarah looked squarely at Esther again and said, "I need to move for a while; my feet are sound asleep. Esther, shall we go out and bring water for them all?"

"Here—take a pitcher, each of you," Mother said, and hurried to the kitchen to take her best and largest ones from the shelf.

The moment they were out of sound of the house, Sarah said, "Esther, I have seen him! Yesterday!"

The way she spoke the words it was as if they were

set to a tune in her mind, a tune as quick and gay as the one about the mockingbirds.

Esther could not even speak. Sarah said, "Here, hold the pitcher and I will pump while I tell you. Then nobody will notice us."

While the clear water came pouring out, she said, "He wants to see you as soon as he can. He said to tell you how sorry he was not to have said good-by. He said that if he had come to say good-by to you—and to me"— she forgot to pump for a second—"he would not have been able to go at all."

"Why *did* he go?" Esther cried. "Did he say why he went?"

"He will tell you himself," Sarah said. And then she told where she had seen him. "Esther, I was at that farm sale, with Father and Mother. Your father was there too. It was a big crowd. I had only been there a little while and was standing behind Mother when a little boy came through the crowd toward me and asked, 'Is your name Sarah Yoder?' I said, Yes, it was, surprised because he wasn't an Amish boy. Then he said, 'Here is a letter then,' and slipped it into my hand and went away, toward the barn."

Esther could not wait for the next part to be told, but cried out, "And the letter was from Dan!"

"I could not imagine what it was," Sarah said. "I

turned my back and opened it. I knew Dan's writing. And I read it as soon as everybody was busy with the next sale."

She stopped speaking and Esther said, "What did **it** say?"

Sarah's face was very pink and the pitcher was full and running over. "It said—Esther, I know every word. I have read it over a hundred times since yesterday. It said, 'Dear Sarah, I came to the sale hoping some of the People would be here. But especially you. I am waiting now among the wagons, behind the barn. If you can make an excuse I would like to speak with you. Your friend, Dan.' "

"So—" Esther breathed, "you hurried to the wagons—"

"I had to wait until I was sure nobody would notice where I went. I could tell from the auctioneer's voice just how the sale was going. And—yes, I hurried, Esther, as fast as I could—" She laughed. "Perhaps we had better stop pumping. We have filled these pitchers forty times already. Your mother will say we are wasting the earth's water."

"And you saw him," Esther said. She reached out and touched Sarah's hand, as if to touch Sarah now would bring Dan close at once.

"He wants to see you, Esther. I told him you were going to the school now."

"But isn't he coming home?" Esther cried.

"He will tell you about that," Sarah said.

"But *when?*"

"When he can. As soon as he can. When you see him, you will know why he doesn't come here right away."

Mother came to the door of the kitchen. "We must go in now, Esther, or they will know we have secrets," Sarah said.

"Sarah, where is he? Is he far away?"

"Not far now," Sarah said. "Now we must go in."

As they came near the house, carrying the pitchers carefully, she began to talk of other things.

But for Esther the whole world had changed. When she helped to pass the cake and lemonade she felt as if she must dance instead of walk through the doors. When she looked at Sarah and met her eyes, quickly, she wanted to shout out loud. When she heard Sarah laughing and talking now, she understood.

So everything was going to be all right again. She did not yet know how, or where, or when. But it hardly mattered, for Sarah had said "soon." Monday? Tuesday? Wednesday? *When?*

How could she wait through all the preaching of another Sunday to go back to school and wait for Dan to come?

When the quilt was finished at last it was nearly dark. Rows of yellow-topped buggies appeared from both directions to take the women home. Sarah's father came, and her own brothers. She turned to wave to Esther. She was, in her own grown-up way, as beautiful as Mary, Esther thought. How lovely she would be if she could wear pink—and blue—and green.

Ruth touched her arm and said, "Esther, will you help me to hold the quilt up for Hans to see it?"

How happy Ruth was! She held the beautiful quilt in her hands tenderly, as if it might vanish at any moment. Yet it was thick and well-made and strong, with thousands of stitches that went entirely through and made the shapes of birds and flowers and twigs and leaves on the other side.

"It is a very pretty quilt," Hans said. But he hardly looked at it, as a matter of fact, Esther noticed. He looked at Ruth, and she did not seem to mind in the least.

So—it was not sad to be in love after all, Esther thought.

~9~

DAN—WITH BUTTONS

At Monday, during recess, she was playing jacks with Mary when it happened. She had been watching the road; every little while she glanced up. Yet when it really happened she was not ready in the least.

One of the boys called her name. "Esther! Here is your brother. He wants to talk to you."

She was on her feet so quickly that the jacks scattered off the steps, swept away by her long skirt, and the ball went bouncing across the ground.

"Why, Esther—" Mary cried, quite cross.

But Esther did not hear. She was looking toward the road, out by the bridge where a strange man stood. It was not Dan, after all. But yes— Yes! She forgot Mary and the jacks and the ball and everything. She lifted her skirts to keep from stumbling as she ran.

He looked different, except for his wide smile, as she came running. His hair was cut short and was combed without any bangs at all, so that his face looked long and strange. He wore no wide-brimmed hat or any hat at all. And he had buttons on his coat. Three neat buttons fastened it right down the middle of his front. He swung her off her feet and held her close against his buttons, laughing.

"Esther, you're so *big!*" he said.

"You have buttons!" That silly thing was all she could think of at first. So much gladness, and she said only that one silly thing.

Yet she knew from his face that he understood.

"Can we walk down the road a little, and sit on the grass?" he asked. "I must talk with you. Sarah said she would tell you I was coming."

She said nothing but kept her hand in his and they began to walk. Once she glanced back to see where Mary was, suddenly remembering. Mary was standing by the step, watching, and when she saw Esther look at her she waved. So it would be all right.

The feeling of Dan's hand, hard and big, was as familiar to her as the hollow where she always lay, snug, in her own bed. "We will sit here; then you can hear the bell in time," said Dan. He sat on the grass with his feet on the flat stones the stream made when there was water running by the road in the springtime. As one might look at a beautiful gift, he turned, then, and looked at her, from her head to her feet.

"You look well," he said. "Esther, you are growing up now. Do you like the school?"

"Oh, yes!" How freely and gladly she could say it to him! "And I wanted to tell you—" She stopped. First he should tell her, for he was the one who had been away, nobody knew where. "Dan, first tell me where you went. Father burned your letter in the stove," she said.

"He did? I expected he would." Dan looked over her head and far down the road, in the direction of home. "I knew he couldn't possibly understand how I felt. He never did. Sometimes I thought if I could tell him—"

Esther's face felt suddenly swollen and her wrists went weak where they lay upon her lap. The very words from her very own thoughts! Perhaps a thought itself could be The First Step Away. For a minute she felt frightened—and of Dan himself, as if he had become somebody else for a time, a stranger after all. A horse was coming along the road and she stood quickly up. If it should be Father riding by!

But it was not Father. The horseman, a man she had never before seen, nodded as he went past them and disappeared.

Dan was looking at her. "Why are you afraid?" he

asked. "Am I so different?" There was a sad strained look on his face below his combed-back hair.

"Oh, no. No, Dan!" she cried, and flung herself against him, against buttons and all, and began to cry as she had never cried before in all her life. He let her cry awhile and then got a handkerchief out of his pocket and told her, in a gentle voice much like Father's, to blow her nose. "It's because I prayed you'd come back, and you did," she said, and blew her nose hard and smiled. "I knew you were coming before Sarah told me."

Then he laughed, throwing his head back in the old glad way. "You and Sarah!" he said. "All that praying. And of course Mother too. How could a man stay away with all that praying pulling him back every day?" Then he took hold of her arms and looked at her, straight in the face the way Mother did when she meant to tell something so important it was never to be forgotten. "Esther, I think I want to come home again."

She could not answer. Such a gladness came over her that it was as if her very skin was different. As if she might be sprouting little feathers, maybe; she actually felt the stirring of something at the roots of her hair.

"I don't know whether Father will ever let me come back," he said. "Sarah isn't sure he will, and John—

Well, John is sure he won't. And the Yoders will be angry because I came and spoke to Sarah behind their backs."

"Why don't you go there and knock on the front door?" she asked.

"I did, Esther. Sarah thought I should, and so last night I did. But Brother Yoder refused to let me in."

Dan himself! The one everybody loved, the one everybody looked at with pride. Esther imagined how terrible it must have been to stand there at the house of those old friends, people Dan had known since he was born, and have the door closed in his face.

"It was different with John," Dan said. "I went to his place afterward. It's the way he said, Esther, some of the Amish are changing but some of the old ones keep fighting to keep everything the same. Do you remember hearing at church about Shunning?"

Shunning? She remembered the word and that it was something very bad. But she was not at all sure what was bad about it.

"Of course I have heard of it all my life," Dan said, "and knew it was how the Amish began. John says they were with the Mennonites once, in the beginning. They all came together from Switzerland and from the Rhineland in Germany. Hundreds of years ago, now.

But do you know why they broke away, the Amish, and followed Jacob Amman?" He did not really expect her to answer, but only paused and went on thoughtfully. "I had never thought about it much, I'm afraid. But John told me plenty of stories. He said the Amish were called Amman's Men at first, and they broke away because they believed as he did—when somebody did something wrong they believed that one should be *shunned entirely.* Nobody among the People should ever so much as speak to him or nod to him, ever again. Or they would be shunned too."

She sat gazing at him as she listened. He stopped and sighed, and she said, "So that's why Father burned your letter."

"Yes. That was why. There are always some old ones who try to keep everything the same. It is usually the young ones, as John said, who want to make changes. The thing is—" He was frowning. "Esther, there are so many good things to keep! When you go away you begin to see them. When I came back to this place—" He waved his hand, as if to include the whole valley along the road and all the farms lying beautiful and snug after the harvest. October was red and yellow everywhere. Wheat stubble was golden; buckwheat was dark red; new winter wheat was already growing

green. Barns stood high and square with silos like ancient towers beside them.

"You remember when Jacob's barn burned, Esther?" Dan asked. "A new one was built for him in a week, remember, and filled with hay. That could only happen here—with the People. That's one of the things I have learned since I went away."

She had never thought such a thing was strange, but only natural.

"When Reuben's leg was broken, we harvested his

crops," Dan said. He looked at her, shaking his head. "I knew all that, but now I know it better. Some of us are stubborn and have to see things with our own eyes, away from here. John said he had to see things too, when he was young. The Thomases, he said."

"Doubting Thomases." She agreed; she had heard that old story, many many times. Thomas would not believe Jesus had come back to life until he saw for himself. The preacher always ended the story with what Jesus said, and now it came to her and she knew what it meant and why it was preached so often. The ones who had believed without seeing were the best.

"Yes, I was a Doubting Thomas," Dan said. "And in many ways I haven't changed, Esther, even yet. But a man is foolish if he tries to begin entirely new, by himself."

He sat gazing over the land in silence for a time, at the way the hills swelled gently up and gently down again. "I have missed seeing you every day; I wanted you to know it," he said. "And Mother. Yes, and Father too. I even began to dream of apple pies; when I passed the wild apple trees on the way here I could smell them cooking."

The bell rang. Instantly Dan stood up. But Esther said, "Dan—are you coming home? Are you?" Now she wasn't sure of anything at all.

"I would like to, if I could come in the right way," he said. "Sarah thinks she knows how I can do it. She says you will help me."

His voice asked a question. Help him? She did not have to say the words, but only looked up at him. He took her hand and they began to walk. "Hurry," he said. "I'm afraid I've made you late already."

The children had all gone in, and the teacher stood on the steps, watching.

"Dan, how can I help?" Esther asked, panting. "You'll be here when I come out— No, Father will be here! Dan, at noon. At recess again—"

"Yes," he said. "Now, hurry—"

"Promise, Dan!"

"Tomorrow," he said, and gave her a little push and called to the teacher, "I'm sorry! I've made my sister late—"

The teacher smiled and waved at him as if she remembered him very well. She waited until Esther was inside before she followed.

The moment Esther was in her seat Mary turned to her. "Is that your brother? He's so handsome!" she said. "But he wears clothes like anybody." Her voice asked a question.

"He's been Away," Esther said. She knew Mary could not understand all this word *Away* could mean, but there was no other way to say it.

"My big brother Jack went away too," Mary said. "He went to the Army and when he came back he had a big mustache! But everybody laughed so hard he shaved it off again."

"Quiet now! Let's settle down, please," the teacher said.

So Mary had a big brother too. No wonder she understood everything. Her brother had even gone Away, and to the Army, which was a terrible thing to do. Esther wondered if Mary's father had objected to the Army as much as her own Father objected to The World. So when they were looking at the books on the library shelf the next hour, she asked, "Was your

father angry and ashamed because your brother went
Away to the Army?"

Mary looked absolutely amazed. "Angry and
ashamed? Why? Jack *had* to go, just like everybody
else. And he got to be First Class right away. Why,
Esther, Daddy was as proud as he could be!"

How was it possible to understand?

On the way home with Father that afternoon, Esther
tried hard to think of something to say. But everything
seemed wrong. She was so afraid she would give away
such a huge important secret that she held the tip of
her tongue tight between her teeth.

Father looked down at her after a time and said,
"Do you feel well today?"

"Oh, yes! Thank you!" she said, and caught her
tongue again.

"Did school go well?"

"Yes, very well."

"I thought you seemed worried."

Her heart began to beat in that hard way and she
had a pain in her side all of a sudden as if she had
been running too fast. "No," she said, but it didn't
sound true at all.

"Have you been wondering any more?" he asked.

She sat still for a long moment, staring ahead over

the horse, right between its two bobbing ears and down the road. Now was the time to tell him if she hadn't promised. She wanted to tell so much that it was as if her very blood must start bursting out of her mouth if she didn't. But she bit hard and really tasted blood on her tongue. Father sat silent too. When she looked up at him at last she saw that he too was staring down the road. His eyes looked shiny and blank as eyes will look when they stare at nothing. "It seems, for some of us, there has to be a time to wonder," he said at last.

Some of *us*— She could hardly believe her ears. Father too? Surely Father himself had never wondered! Perhaps it would be all right for her to tell him about Dan, after all. But before this thought could even begin to make her glad, Father went on speaking in a voice that expected no answer.

"Wondering is all right in the time of it, Esther. But the time should pass. If you tell me and your Mother what it is you wonder about, we can explain to you."

Well, I am wondering about Dan. She longed to say it and see what Father would say and how he would look. But she knew he was talking about Dan already. Dan had not stopped wondering soon enough. He hadn't stopped with wondering about buttons, for instance, but had to get some and wear them himself, down his very own front where everybody could see them. He hadn't stopped with wondering about hair, but let somebody shear his own from his head the way Samson was shorn by Delilah. Dan had gone so much farther than wondering that she knew it could never be explained. Perhaps it could never be forgiven now.

Then she thought about Mary. Was now the time to say to Father, "There is a girl at school named Mary, who is very kind and good to me. I have been wondering if it is all right for her to be my friend." But she could not bring the words to her lips. She did not want Father explaining anything about Mary. If there was something evil in Mary and in her kindness and her pretty hair and her pretty ways, she did not even want to know it.

They came to the gate and Mother was waiting as always with her kind face and her warm firm hands. Ham was cooking and smelled so wonderful that it made Esther's mouth fill with spit like a puppy's. Dan loved ham better than anything, she remembered, except apple pies.

"Mother, I smell ham!" she cried. "May I have a lot in my lunch tomorrow?" When Dan came, she would have saved some for him.

There were little pies for supper too. Esther did not eat hers but laid it in her lap when nobody was looking. Tomorrow there would be another one in her lunch and she and Dan could eat them together.

～ 10 ～

MORE ABOUT DAN

With Dan, it was wonderful. He was there when she came out for recess and stayed to eat lunch with her at noon. How pleased he was with the ham and the little pie!

"Nobody but our Mother can make ham taste like this," he said. "Nobody else makes such apple pies." He looked sad when he said it, and picked up a crumb of piecrust that had dropped upon his clothes. "Are there a great many apples this year?" he asked. He put the crumb tenderly upon his tongue.

Esther told him about the apples. About the berries and the pears and cherries. About the new little pigs. About the cows he knew by name and about each new calf. About the chickens and ducks and turkeys and the great new geese. And about the horses too, especially about his own horse who refused to answer to the new name Father had given him. And about the fine workhorses he had taken to the Fair.

Then it was her turn to ask questions. She asked

every single question right out, without worrying whether it was wrong or right to ask it. Dan answered in the same way, looking at her sometimes to see how his answers seemed to her. Sometimes he gazed off down the road, chewing nervously on the sweet tips of the old grass growing around him.

"Dan, where did you go that day, from the Fair?"

To this question she had wanted an answer so long that she held her breath to hear it begin.

"There was a man there," Dan said, "who liked the way I handled the horses. He said I handled horses better than anybody he ever saw in his life. 'Better than myself!' he said. We got to be friends the first day, and then— Well, that last day I was getting ready to take our horses home, and I had all the blue ribbons, you remember. This man's name was Carpenter, and he was a good fellow. He said, 'Dan, I'd give a good deal for a man like you on my place. You would handle my horses. Nothing else.' He told me about the string he had. Fifty horses, Esther, and some of those I had seen were very fine."

He broke off a whole bunch of grass and chewed it all together into a lump as if he had become a horse himself with all that thinking about horses.

"I knew Father would never let me do such a thing. Not if I asked on my knees. So I decided to go for a while, and send him a letter. That man offered me more money for one month than we have made sometimes for all our hay put together!"

"How wonderful!" Esther said, proudly. "So you bought this good coat with buttons."

Dan looked at her without smiling. "Yes," he said. "But not for a while. At first I meant to come back before too long, but John wrote to me about what Father said. He told me Father never wanted to see me again."

She nodded, knowing it was true as John had said.

"So then, right away, I got one of those automobiles," Dan said. "An old one Mr. Carpenter had driven a long time."

"Dan, not an automobile of your own!"

"Yes, it was mine. This man's place was a long way from town. Near Erie, not far from the big lake. I got the automobile before I even got new clothes. But soon I got the other things too, because it made people laugh to see me in my plain clothes, running that automobile at the same time. Then—" He waited awhile, as if this was something really hard to tell. "This man had a daughter too."

"Oh!" Poor Sarah! Esther's heart stopped in her breast.

"She was pretty, with yellow hair like that girl in

pink you were with when I came. It was because **of** her I got the clothes and everything."

Esther could not look at him, she did not know why. Something was strange and fierce in his voice; it was not Dan's voice at all.

"Well, a fellow has to learn!" he said. His voice sounded as if he had been eating green apples for half a day.

"Didn't she love you back?" Esther asked. It seemed impossible; how could any girl in the world not love Dan if he loved her? Every Plain Girl anywhere near his age looked at him with hope. Esther knew it, and everybody else knew it too.

"Maybe she did," Dan said. "With those girls, it's hard to tell. You see, those girls—" His face began to burn. Under Esther's clear gaze, his blood rose through his throat and into his cheeks and into his forehead. "They go with lots of different fellows, sometimes a new one every night in the week. I told her I didn't like it at all." His voice was full of pain, and his face. "Well, she laughed at me. She told everybody. Her father laughed about it one day and asked if I expected a girl of *his* to go steady with me. So I said Yes. I said, Yes, that she had—" Dan lay back in the grass and looked up at the clouds that were all stirred up within themselves exactly the way Esther felt inside herself at that moment. "I said she had kissed me already. And it was true."

"Oh!" Esther said again. Her heart was beating just inside both her ears. What a triumph, for Dan to be able to tell *that* to the girl's father! "So then," she asked eagerly, "what did he say then?"

Dan's voice was slow and hard and far away. "He laughed at me," he said. "Then I knew that things were too different with those people, after all. That girl was only one thing. Her father didn't always keep his word. I got so I couldn't really believe anything he said—and sometimes he forgot to pay me. He said he forgot; I couldn't tell whether it was true. And that automobile—every time I drove it something went wrong. It was bad machinery."

"So now where is it?" Esther asked.

Dan's voice was angry. "It is a piece of junk. That man was a piece of junk too; he thought of nothing but money. Even his horses were nothing but money to him. So I wrote him a letter finally, the way I wrote one to Father, and came away without seeing him afterward. And that girl—" He lay very still, looking up. "I didn't write a letter to her. I thought I would, but when I started to write, there was nothing to say."

Esther stared down at her hands, folded in her lap. At last Dan reached out and lifted her chin and looked tenderly down into her face. "Do you know what I did instead?" he asked. "I thought about Sarah. I couldn't get her out of my mind—how pretty she was, but more than that, how well she understood everything. I began wanting to see her so much I could hardly wait. I heard about a farm sale and thought she might be there and I might see her."

"And you did. She told me."

"Yes, I did. It was her idea that I should come to her place last night—just to see what happened. We

have a special place to leave letters, Sarah and I—"
He was smiling again and his face was red. "You see
that old tree at the crossroads, the one with the woodpecker holes in it? Sarah and I used to leave notes there
sometimes, when we were both in school. When I was
away I often thought of that old tree."

The bell had begun to ring. But Esther hardly heard
it. "Dan, how are you coming home again?" she asked.

He did not answer directly but pulled her to her
feet and hurried her down the road toward the school.

"Father will want you to come back—when he
knows—" she panted. "He said the other day that
everybody—wondered for a while—"

Dan stopped in the road. "Are you sure? *Father* said
that?" he asked.

"I don't remember exactly how he said it. But I
thought that's what he meant. Dan—if only your hair
was long again, and you had another coat!"

"Without buttons," he said.

They found all the children had gone in again, all
but Mary who stood by the steps alone.

"Dan, there are some of your old clothes in Mother's
chest. I could roll them up and put them somewhere,
where you could find them."

"And my hair is growing. Esther, it's surprising how
fast a man's hair will grow. When it costs a whole dol-

lar to have it cut in a shop, you begin to notice how fast."

The teacher came to the door and spoke to Mary, and Mary went in. Then the teacher stood looking at Esther. Her mouth looked cross and tight, and Esther could see how she followed Dan away with her eyes. Once was all right, she seemed to be saying, but *every day* . . .

"I'll see you one day next week," Dan called.

When Esther came to the door she expected a good scolding. But the teacher only said, frowning, "Esther, is there trouble at home?"

"Oh, no!" Esther said, surprised. "No, ma'am! It's going to be all right at home now."

She slipped into her seat. She was so filled with happiness that the seat seemed too small to hold her and all that happiness too. Presently, when she and Mary stood by the shelf of books, Mary asked, "Is your brother going to come every day?"

"No. Not until next week now. Tomorrow—" She stopped. Was Mary like the girl Dan knew where he had been working? But no, it was impossible. Mary would never laugh at anybody, she knew it. "Tomorrow we can play together again," she said. As she spoke, it came to her that now she could ask Dan about Mary. There wouldn't be any trouble about asking

Dan such a thing. It would be easy. How wonderful to look into his face and say, "There's a girl at school—the one you saw in pink—"

The next day and the next she and Mary played. She was getting better and better. The jacks were familiar in her hands, now, like little friends. The ball did as she wanted it to do and never bounced the wrong direction because she knew about all the cracks in the step. Once two other girls played with them, and Esther and Mary were partners and won the game.

∾ 11 ∾

A WEDDING—AND A FRIEND

It did not seem long between Dan's visits because for a while everything was too exciting at home. What a shame for Dan to miss the wedding! He would have liked teasing Hans on his wedding day and tossing the last bridegroom over the fence.

Esther brought a note to the teacher asking to be excused on Tuesday. The teacher read it and smiled at her. "A wedding at your house!" she said. "How wonderful, Esther. Is it a sister who is being married?"

"No, it is my Aunt Ruth." To herself Esther said, "But next year it will be my brother." If only Dan's hair would grow faster, he wouldn't have to wait a whole year to marry Sarah. But when he came by the school that day his hair was only looking rather foolish and raggedy around his ears.

"I hate missing all that good food," he said. "Sarah says she will put a piece of pie in that woodpecker tree."

Esther laughed. "The woodpeckers would eat it."

"They are too smart, those birds," Dan said. "I suppose I will have to wait for my own wedding." He sighed even though he spoke so lightly, and Esther knew how much he would like to come.

The night before the wedding, Esther thought only of Ruth. Everything was packed in her big chest, ready to go with her and Hans when the feast was over. Ruth sat on her bed and put a few last firm stitches in her blue dress. Beside her lay her starched white apron and the white kerchief for her head. "Think of it, Esther," she said, "until my funeral now I will never wear a white apron or kerchief again!"

It seemed too bad to Esther that a girl must wear black after she was married, but she could see that Ruth did not mind very much. She would rather wear black and be with Hans than to wear white and be without him.

At dawn the house was filled with wonderful smells of cooking. Nobody would believe how much food there was unless he saw it. Chickens and sides of beef and a great roasting goose and hams and cheeses and everything to make a full dinner around them. Then there were cakes, white and dark and in between. And pies by the dozens, apple and peach and apricot and cherry and pumpkin and mince. Besides cookies and homemade ice cream.

Sarah came early to help. It was as wonderful to have a secret with Sarah as it was to have a secret with Mary. "Are you saving a pie for the woodpeckers?" she asked, and they giggled together.

Before noon wagons were arriving, one after another. People came from many miles away; the yard was filled with wagons and the barn with horses, and more were lined up on the road. Inside the house there was not enough room for all to sit down and people stood along the walls. But everybody looked happy whether he stood up or sat down, for a wedding is one of the happiest things in all the world.

When Ruth came in with Hans in his new black suit, made by his mother, there was a little hush. Even the children were quiet for a while. The preachers took the bride and groom upstairs to tell them about the duties of husbands and wives to each other, and the service began. Presently Ruth and Hans came down again, looking very serious indeed, and sat on the front bench. It was very like Sunday, then, with sermons and songs, but all the songs were different for they were special songs for marriages.

When it ended, Ruth and Hans led the way to the feast. Then the fun began! You would have thought from the piles of food and the busy women bringing plates and platters and bowls back and forth that they

were feeding the whole State of Pennsylvania. Once Esther noticed Mother following Sarah with her eyes; it was a sad look and Esther knew Mother was thinking about Dan and wishing he were here. If only she could tell Mother why Sarah was happy again. But of course she could not. "Well, Esther," Mother said, catching her eye, "some day we will be having such a feast for *you!*"

Hans' buggy was shining clean with new black paint on the wheels. His horse, beautifully groomed, waited between the shafts. Ruth's chest was carried out and packed behind the seat. As dusk fell, Ruth and Hans ran to the buggy and leaped in and drove away, with everybody shouting and waving after them.

Esther turned to see Sarah beside her. "Esther, Dan wonders why I must be married at home," Sarah said. "It is hard for me to tell him why I want it to be like this."

"Maybe he doesn't want to wait until next November!" Esther said.

Then Sarah looked happier, and they went in to help with the dishes.

117

The very next day Dan rode by the school on a fine horse. He was in high spirits. "I found a job right away," he said. "It's easy to find work on the farms. Esther, do you think my hair will be long enough by Christmas?"

Christmas seemed a long time away, but Esther agreed with Dan that it would be a very good time to come home. There would be many sermons spoken about kindness and about wanderers; every window would have a candle in it. When she spoke of the candles Dan nodded and said, "I will come on Christmas Eve."

"Just before supper is put on the table." Esther could imagine Father trying to turn Dan away when Mother had just put supper on the table!

"You'd better put those clothes out before snow," Dan said. "It's a long way to come from where I work, especially at night." They decided that she would roll the clothes into a bundle and drop them out of her window the very next Sunday night. His old shoes and all, for Dan wanted to be dressed exactly as he had been before he went away. "Sarah says nothing at all must be different," he said. His laugh sounded strange. "I tell her it is a good thing the brim of my hat is wide, to hide my thoughts."

At first Esther thought she should hide the clothes

in advance, behind the sheds or in the barn. But Dan said No, it would be too easily discovered if she did anything at all by day. And the animals would make a fuss if he came near in the night. "How will you get into that chest without Mother knowing?" he asked. "Esther, I don't want to cause you trouble and worry. I've been bad enough for you already."

Bad? She had to tell him over and over that now he was coming home again, it was all good. "And about the chest," she said. "When Mother was in the chicken coop the other day, I looked at the things. I know exactly where they are because I tucked them in a corner all together. Dan—" His face, she had noticed more and more lately, was not much like Father's; it was like Mother's, especially his blue eyes. "Why do you think Mother didn't give those clothes away? Whenever something is too small for me, she gives it to some family with girls younger than I am. But those clothes of yours she never gave away. I saw her put them in the chest."

Dan looked troubled. "Maybe she thought nobody would want his boys to wear my old clothes!" he said.

Esther hadn't thought of that, but now she saw it might be true. With the Plain People, wearing was one of the most important things. Now, she thought, is the time to ask Dan my question.

"Dan—" She had expected it would be easier than it was. If only that girl hadn't been so cruel to him, so he might now expect every pretty girl to be the same. "I must ask you something. I wanted to ask Father, but I couldn't. Besides, I knew his answer already."

"Yes?" Dan looked at her flushed face and away again. "Esther, aren't you young to be worrying about questions? If you know the answer—" He paused. "Why ask it?"

"I know Father's answer," she said. "But it keeps asking itself in my mind." She looked up at him. "It's like that about buttons and souls."

It was a strange thing. As soon as she said it, there was a silence between them. Everything went still and strange the way it does sometimes in the night when the wind stops blowing.

At last Dan turned to her and said, "Well?"

She still sat looking down at her hands.

"The bell will be ringing," he said, and reached out and put his arm around her shoulders. "Do you want to ask that question today?"

She wasn't sure now that she did. But there was Mary, back in the schoolyard, and Mary too was waiting for an answer. She looked up. "Dan—" Then she said it. "There's a girl at school who is my friend. That pretty girl you noticed. She sits in front of me and we play together and talk together. And we write letters back and forth now, every day." It began to come faster now she was started, and she knew she must finish entirely before the bell. "She likes my long dresses and my bonnet and my apron and even my high shoes. We want to trade some day—"

His face was shocked. Really shocked.

"Just at school!" she said. "Just for a little while!"

For the first time he looked like Father, and for the first time she had something in her besides love for him. How could he look like that after all the things he himself had done? With his hair half-grown the way it was now, he looked very silly, to tell the truth. It hung down over his ears, neither plain nor unplain but something silly in between that was like nothing at all. "There is a pink dress," she said, "and sandals with buckles and a petticoat with a ruffle all around the edge and lace on it. I saw the petticoat—she showed it to me—"

He looked as if somebody had hit him over the head with a stone. Daniel. She could hardly believe it. She had expected he would understand entirely.

"I see," he said after a time. But what it was he saw she didn't learn just then; the bell was ringing. He stood up quickly and said, "Esther, I'll think about this awhile. I don't know— I never thought about such a thing with you."

Before he had finished she was running back toward school, running with her long skirts held up in her hands to let her go fast down the road and over the bridge and up the hill. Mary stood waiting as always. She laughed when she saw Esther running so fast. "You're not going to be late," she said, and held out her hand as always before and they went into the schoolroom as before and found their places together. Esther could not speak. In her throat was a burning lump that kept rising up and seemed to close off even her nose.

"What's the matter? Is something wrong?" Mary asked.

"Please—" Esther leaned close over her desk for fear she would begin to cry right here in the middle of school.

Mary sat still in front of her and did not turn around again at all. But her elbow, with its dimple and the little puffed sleeve above it, was moving, and presently she turned just enough to drop a note on Esther's desk.

What would it say this time? Now Esther had a wonderful little secret pile of Mary's letters, far back in the corner of her desk. They were tied together in a bundle, with a piece of silver string she had found along the street one day in town. Her fingers trembled as she unfolded the new one. How neat and plain Mary's letters were! The lines did not wobble in the least; they went straight along, one after the other. Mary was the best writer in the class. Sometimes the teacher posted her exercises on the board, for an exhibit of how they should be done.

Dear Friend Esther:
I am sorry you are feeling bad. I wish I could help. Recess is not fun when you're not there. Shall we be Bosom Friends?

Love,
Mary.

Bosom Friends. Esther knew what Bosom Friends were. The Twos. Those with secrets together. Those who saved each other places. Those who were always on the same side and chose each other.

She read the letter over and over. If Mary had expected her letter to take away the lump in Esther's throat, she was mistaken. It only got bigger and bigger until Esther felt she would never swallow again. It was like a great solid lump of tears, like a cloud swollen with rain. If only she could cry awhile, it might go away. But nobody could burst into tears in the middle of a class in arithmetic.

She sat still and tried to think about the problems. After a while, the teacher asked her a question about one of them. And to her surprise she was able to answer. Her answer was right. Afterward, she felt better.

How should she answer Mary's note? The last hour of the day, when she was supposed to be reading a book, she put a piece of paper in the book instead and began to write:

Dear Mary:
    I would like to be your Bosom Friend. . . .

She must write what was true. Hadn't Mary written "I wish I could help," besides all those other kind things before? Mary was not like that girl Dan knew. Not at all. Esther knew this so strongly and surely that her fingers became firm and certain on the pencil. Then she sat reading what she had written.

Dear Mary:
    I would like to be your Bosom Friend. If you will wear your pink dress Monday, we will change at recess.
                    Your Bosom Friend,
                        Esther.

Dan had nothing to do with Mary. Father had nothing to do with Mary either. Nor Mother. Not anybody. Bosom Friends were friends because friendship happened to them, like breathing air and drinking water. Friendship was the most beautiful thing in the world! She folded the letter carefully and reached into her desk and broke off a little piece of the silver thread to tie it.

How beautiful Mary's smile was when she had read it and turned around! "All right," she said. When they stood up to march again, she squeezed Esther's hand. They walked with their hands linked between them all the way out of the schoolhouse and down the steps and halfway to the big orange bus.

"See you Monday!" Mary said, so everybody could hear.

Monday was their secret. Esther laughed and answered, "See you Monday," but nobody but the two of them knew what Monday really meant.

Esther stood watching the bus until it disappeared. She was filled with happiness. She was like a soap bubble with colors floating through her in every direction. She wanted to sing. She wanted to laugh out loud. She wanted to lift her skirt and dance. Or run or skip. But instead she turned and walked back to the steps and sat down to wait for Father's buggy to appear down the road. When he came and she sat beside him, he didn't seem to notice anything new about her, or different.

"How did it go at school today?" he asked after a time.

"Very well," she said. She tried to keep her voice from singing.

If he only knew how very well! she thought.

~ 12 ~

ESTHER DOES
SOME WORK AT NIGHT

That Sunday, Esther had so many special thoughts to think that it was hard to concentrate on the speaking and the singing. She planned over and over in her mind exactly how she would manage about Dan's clothes. When Sarah smiled at her again, as before, in that we-have-a-secret way, she wondered whether Sarah knew about the clothes. Did Sarah know it would be tonight?

Then an interesting thought came to her: how did Dan and Sarah meet without the Yoders knowing? How would they manage in the day? Yet how would they manage in the *night?* It was exciting to think about in the middle of a meeting.

It was going to be hard enough just to drop Dan's bundle out of the window. She must stay awake until Father and Mother were sound asleep, even if she had to sit up in the cold to manage it. Then she must creep into the hall without a sound and open the chest. She had tried the lid and it made a squeak every time, but if she lifted it slowly the squeak was long and low instead of quick and loud.

Dan needed his heavy coat, so the bundle would be very big. She was glad she had thought of the coat. The shoes could be wrapped in the very middle, so they would make no clatter as they fell to the ground.

If Father should hear it fall! Or Mother. She could imagine their voices in the dark. "I heard something . . ." "Yes, so did I!" "What can it be?" It was terrible to think of Father sitting bolt upright in the dark. "I had better go and find out . . ."

But they were less apt to hear the bundle fall than they were to hear her steps if she tried creeping down the stairs with it.

Every time her thoughts came to the very moment of letting the bundle fall, she began to shiver. They wouldn't hear. She would be too careful. Yet if they did, what then? She knew Dan would be as quiet as possible when he came. Of course she would hear him herself because she would be listening.

How long the speakings were today! She was afraid there might be something special said about secrets and sin, but there was not. It was all about harvesting and about souls. So it seemed to her that what she meant to do was all right with God. She was relieved. He under-

stood how important it was for Dan to come home again. He was arranging things the way he had arranged them for The Prodigal Son. It would have been very nice if the speaking today had told about The Prodigal Son, she thought. She wanted Father to think about it many times before Christmas Eve.

After church had ended for the day, the men stayed a long time, laughing and talking together. It was good for Father to enjoy himself today, Esther decided, so he would sleep well tonight. But when he slept well he was apt to snore she remembered. Maybe he would snore so loud tonight that Mother would stay awake! Oh, dear— But then, on the other hand, maybe he would snore so loud Mother couldn't hear anything else. All the way home through the cold starry evening, Esther's thoughts went one way and then another.

After they got home, Mother did all sorts of things. She set some yeast in potato water for the next day's baking. She mended one of Father's heavy working socks, for he needed it, he said, and to prove it soaked a blistered heel in the washbasin. "Esther, tomorrow is school again. You must go to bed." Mother's voice was never cross, but could be as strong as Father's in its own way.

Tomorrow is school again. Esther had been so concerned with tonight she had pushed tomorrow away. Yet tomorrow was *the* Monday—*the* Monday Mary would wear her pink dress.

It was almost too much to think about as Esther kissed her Mother's forehead and said good night. What if Mother knew that before tomorrow came, her own son Daniel would creep from the road among the trees and come closer to the house, and closer, until he was so close she could almost hear him breathing if she listened? What if she knew that tomorrow her own daughter Esther would wear a bright pink dress? It was terrible to be filled with secret thoughts. But it was wonderful too. Esther felt so alive, so *real*, that her very toes were tingling in her shoes.

When she undressed, she left her heavy stockings on. She could creep to the chest very silently in those stockings. When she got into bed she lay stiff and straight. Usually she curled up into a bow and felt soft everywhere, like a bird in a nest. But not tonight. If she were comfortable she might go off to sleep without even knowing it. Above everything she must not go to sleep.

How terrible it would be if Dan came all that distance, tied his horse as far off as the old bridge lest it be heard on the road, and then found his bundle wasn't there! He would search under her window, beneath the leafless vines. Under the lilac trees. He would look and look. Then he would go away, knowing she had failed him, thinking she was angry because of that question he didn't answer. Maybe he would even decide not to come home again, after all.

Her bones began to ache from holding them so tight together. Her eyes wanted to close. But downstairs Mother was still talking. Then Father. What was it they talked about, on and on and on? Did they talk so long every night? Perhaps they did, and she was never awake to notice. They talked now and then as they came upstairs, something about chickens. She heard everything they did, their shoes coming to the floor, their lying down at last. Father yawning. Mother sighing. At last, at last Father snoring!

Slowly she slipped out of the covers. The bed creaked if she moved quickly, so she turned herself gradually from the covers like a snake from its old skin. How cold the floor was! And *it* creaked too, something she had never noticed before. Even the door creaked when she opened it, and she stood still for a while before she went into the hall, shivering and listening. It isn't only your ears you hear with, she thought, for she seemed to be listening all over, clear to the soles of her feet. Even her toes were curled tightly down to the floor as if they listened through the boards.

Nothing stirred. But Father was not snoring now— Had she wakened him? Not one sound came from Father or from Mother, either one. Esther waited, holding her breath. Weren't they even *breathing?* They had to, and so did she. She had held her breath so long her face felt swollen like a balloon.

Then she began to hear Father again. First he snored a little short snore, then a little longer one, and then suddenly he gave a snort like a horse! Now she was shivering and listening and laughing all together. He began to breathe steadily again. Gradually he breathed louder—and longer—and then *another* snort! So that was the way Father slept.

She began to move forward again. If only the lid of the chest would not squeak! She lifted it slowly—slowly —slowly—and it did not make a sound. Even if it had, nobody would have heard, for Father was snorting and snoring away as loud as you please. Carefully she lifted the bundle out onto the floor, then lowered the lid again. Carrying Dan's roll of clothes tight against her was comforting; it was a bundle as big as a baby. But Dan would have to air his things a long time to get the mothballs out.

What a relief to be back in her own room again! She closed the door and stood against it, feeling weak, as tired as if she had run up a long hill. While she was standing there, she heard a rustle outside, among the dry leaves. So Dan was there already.

She rushed to the window, almost forgetting to be quiet. For her, Dan was home already. Even though Mother and Father did not know it, her prayers were answered right now, in the middle of the night.

She heard no more sound at all. She reached out and dropped the bundle onto the ground. Still silence. Had she imagined she heard him before? But no— something was moving. Then she heard a whisper, "I've got it!" And she heard him moving away. Nobody else in the world could have heard him, he went so quietly, walking on the grass and the wet leaves.

Until she heard the far-off sound of a horse on the road, she forgot she was cold. Then all of a sudden she was in a shiver that shook her from head to heels. But so happy, so happy! She curled up in a bow as always before, and soon fell asleep.

When she woke up, she was full of a bright sunny feeling. Today. It was today now. What was it she had been dreaming? It was slipping away from her now; it was a kind of pink cloud in her mind, the way Mary had been that first day. But it was something about pink dresses fluttering magically down from a high window, bundles and bundles of pink dresses, and Mary laughing as she tossed them down.

✐ 13 ✐

THE ANSWER

When Father drove her to school, Esther was surprised to see Sarah sitting in front in the Yoder wagon. Father nodded and spoke to her. "You are up early this morning," he said, looking curious. "I thought your family was all too old for school now. Is your father here?"

Sarah made some sort of motion, neither a nod nor a shake of the head. She looked flustered, Esther thought. Girls did not usually drive buggies, but Sarah sat at the side properly, where women usually sat.

Esther knew at once that Sarah must have come alone. And that she must have come to talk to her. But why? What could have happened? Had Dan been caught with the clothes? Hadn't he found them, after all? Her heart seemed to stop in her chest.

Father sat talking for a while, asking Sarah about all of her family as if he had not seen them the day before. Esther thought he would never go away. But soon the school bus appeared down the road, and then, thank goodness, he drove quickly off.

"Esther, I must speak with you," Sarah said. "Dan asked me to come. Here—climb up and sit by me." She saw the question in Esther's eyes and said, with spirit, "Yes, I drove here alone. Dan isn't the only one who sometimes does as he pleases!"

Sarah tucked a quilt about both their knees for the morning was chilly. Then she sat looking out over the horse's head in silence, watching—as Esther did— as the children got out of the bus, one by one. When Mary climbed out she saw Esther at once and waved and smiled. Esther waved back and smiled too.

"Is that your friend?" Sarah asked suddenly.

So Dan had told her about that. "Yes. Her name is Mary," Esther said.

"She's very pretty. What a nice coat and hat!" Sarah said.

Then she turned and looked down at Esther and said, "Dan told me about what you were wondering. I'm ashamed he didn't tell you it was all right about putting on another dress for a while. I told him so. Why shouldn't you change for a day if you are wondering how it is?"

Esther looked up at her gratefully. "I had decided to do it anyway," she said.

There was a little silence between them, but it was a good silence, full of understanding. Sarah was smiling and shaking her head at the same time. "Do you know what Dan said to me? He said he was not at all afraid about being shunned himself. But as soon as he thought about other people he was not sure about anything any more. The trouble, he said, was that it was never just yourself. Soon after he went away he began to think about you, and about his mother, and about me."

That was how it would be with Dan, of course. Always he had been kind to everybody. And to animals. To everybody and everything.

"He said it made him angry sometimes not to be able to think at all without so many people to consider. He kept thinking how unhappy he had made us all."

It was true about the unhappiness, both of them knew it. Esther wondered whether Sarah was remembering the night she came out onto the porch looking sad, to ask if anybody had heard from Dan.

"Dan will never be happy to go on here, being just the same and doing the same things the same way all his life," Sarah said. "I know how he feels, Esther, wanting to do new things. It is all right with me—if we can do some of the old things too."

The first bell began to ring. None of the children had stayed outside today because it was too cold. Even the bell sounded cold up there in the frosty air.

"Dan wanted me to tell you about my best friend, here at school," Sarah said. "She lives in town now and sometimes I go to see her when we go to market. Mother worried about it at first, but now she seems to think it hasn't done me any harm. Well—when we were about your age, or a little older, Esther, I went to this friend's house after school. We played we were ladies. She had old colored dresses and shoes that had heels on them three inches high. Like stilts."

"Oh!" Esther said. She had heard in church how wicked such high shoes were.

"We also painted our mouths red," Sarah said, her voice sounding reckless and gay. "But when I looked into the glass in her mother's room, it scared me half out of my skin. And I began to cry."

Was that how it would feel in a pink dress? Esther wondered. She looked up at Sarah. "What did you do then? Did you wash it off good before you went home?"

"I scrubbed and she scrubbed. My face was sore," Sarah said. "It must have come off entirely because nobody spoke of it. They only scolded me at home for being late from school. We live nearer to the school than you do; I always walked back and forth in good weather."

The last bell was ringing, and Esther began to get out. But Sarah said, "Wait just a little longer, Esther. I spoke to the teacher before you came; it will be all right."

Today Esther did not want to wait to get into school, but she did not say so, of course. She sat back in the seat again, wondering what Mary would be thinking.

"When Dan and John talk about getting machinery to use together," Sarah said, "I feel sometimes exactly the way I felt about the paint on my face. I am afraid. Yet I know it will be all right, all the same. Some of the Amish people in other places are learning to use certain machines now, to make farming better. There are, as I tell Dan, some ways that are good to keep and some ways that are good to throw away."

Her cheeks were very pink from the cold, and she was laughing a little now. "Esther, when Dan wants all the new things and says I want all the old things, do you know what I tell him? *What if I had to invent how to make every pie and every cake and had learned nothing from my mother at all?* How foolish would that be?" Her eyes were sparkling. "Do you know what he said last night? He said the pies had convinced him. He said he was sure he could not make any better pies with a tractor!"

They laughed together.

"When Dan and I have our house and our farm," Sarah said, "you can come there and do as you please. You will bring your little friend to play, then. Would you like to do that?"

Esther nodded. A lightness, a gladness like that other day had filled her to the fingertips.

"Now you must go in," Sarah said. "But, Esther— one more thing—do you know, Dan said he wasn't at all sure of all this until you asked him that question about the pink dress? He never understood his Father's side of it, not at all, until then. The idea of you in a pink dress with those little socks and shoes and all— he said he couldn't seem to make it do in his mind!"

Esther slipped out from the quilt and got down. She reached up to press Sarah's hand and say good-by, though she couldn't think of another thing to say. Because there were too many things that might be said and not any one would do by itself.

"Dan is even willing to have a wedding now," Sarah said. "He says he might even shine that old light in my window."

"Oh, yes, he should do *that!*" Esther cried then, remembering how it had been with Ruth when Hans came in the night.

Sarah picked up the reins, and Esther turned and ran into the school.

Before she had her coat off and onto its hanger in the corner, she turned to look for Mary. She stood frozen, amazed. Mary had not worn the pink dress, after all.

Before Esther was in her seat, Mary had begun to explain. "Esther, I'm so sorry! It was awful—Mother wouldn't let me wear it! She'd put it away in a box with the summer clothes; she said nobody could wear a dress like that in November. And I—" Her eyes looked huge and sad. "I couldn't tell her I wanted to change with somebody. She wouldn't have liked it at all."

Esther sat still.

"This is my prettiest winter dress," Mary said anxiously. It was very pretty indeed, bright green and wooly, all criss-crossed with lines of yellow and red. It had a cunning little belt with three buckles in a row in the middle.

"Don't you like it?" Mary asked.

"Yes. Oh, yes, it's very pretty!"

"We can change anyhow, then," Mary said, relieved. "Can't we?"

The teacher was rapping. "Please, no talking!" she said.

Esther sat absolutely still. No woodcock ever sat more quietly on its nest. It was as if all the worry she had ever known in her life had melted away. There had been the first great shock of disappointment about the dress, but now a wonderful feeling of relief and happiness had come instead. Mary's mother was just the same as her own. Probably Mary's father was like Father too, in certain ways. They decided what could be worn and what couldn't be worn, and when, just as Amish parents did.

Above all— What had Mary said? *I couldn't tell her I wanted to change with somebody.* There were things Mary couldn't say to her mother, and probably to her father. So it was the same whether you were Plain or not. It was only being young and being old. And Dan—now he was between. But getting older, and in love already.

After a time Mary dropped a letter on her desk. She let it lie there for a while. She knew what it would say before she read the words, and she already knew her answer.

Sure enough. When she unfolded the letter she saw that Mary had written the words she expected.

Dear Esther:

I am glad you like this dress too. Shall **we** change the first recess or the second or at noon?

Your Bosom Friend,

Mary.

In writing class, Esther wrote her answer

Dear Mary:

I am sorry your Mother feels like that. So does mine. Can't we be Bosom Friends without changing?

Esther.

It seemed a long time before Mary answered. Esther began to be afraid she was not going to answer at all. She felt worried again; a cold feeling began to creep over her skin. When somebody laughed suddenly she jumped, thinking the laugh was at her. But it wasn't. Nobody was looking at her at all. Not even Mary. Nobody.

But just before recess, Mary turned and dropped another note, with a smile. It was written hurriedly, with no beginning and no ending like the other letters. It had only one word, very big and sure:

YES.

As they formed lines to march, Mary's soft hand found hers and squeezed, hard. They marched out together. Everybody played the same game because it was cold, a running game with the teacher taking charge. But it was as wonderful as if Mary and Esther sat playing together on the step. Mary was a chooser and called Esther's name the very first time around. Esther could lift her skirts and run as fast as any girl in that school. She could laugh as loud. She squealed and cried "Oh, dear!" when she was caught.

14

CHRISTMAS AT HOME

Never in her life had Esther waited for Christmas so eagerly. All the time she was painting Christmas pictures in school, huge yellow stars for the windows and bright red Santa Claus figures for the walls and little green trees to hang from the ceiling on strings, she was thinking about Dan. All the time she helped make decorations and trim the tall school tree, she was thinking about his coming. When the teacher hung Angel Hair on the tree, she wondered how fast Dan's hair had been growing.

Before every meal and every night when she went to bed, she repeated the same prayer: *Help Father to be glad when Dan comes home. Help him to let Dan stay.*

The last afternoon before holidays, gifts were exchanged at school. Everybody drew names from a box, each giving one gift. Esther did not tell the teacher that Amish people gave no gifts, but drew a name in turn; she would bring a bag of Mother's delicious cookies. She knew Mother would let her bring such a thing to school. Another gift she wrapped in secret in her own room and took to school under her coat. It was an apron exactly like the one she wore for Sunday-best. It would look very neat, as white as snow, tied around Mary's waist to protect her pretty dresses. She pinned to it a little note: *Your Bosom Friend wishes you all the joy of Christmas.*

On the package she drew a great yellow star on the tip of a green tree, using the crayons she had at school.

The gift she received in the exchange was a pair of warm black gloves. But just before the day ended, Mary turned around and slipped a small package onto her desk. It was wrapped in shining pink paper that showed reflections like one of the pink baubles on the school tree. A silver card hung from it on a silver string. It said something in print and then, in Mary's familiar writing, "Merry Christmas to my Bosom Friend."

She held it in her hands, admiring it, and Mary laughed and said, "Shake it, Esther. See if you can guess what it is."

It had the same little metal clicking that she had heard so often on the step as the jacks shook together in her hand. It was the same sound she always heard when Mary swung the green mesh bag containing her jacks and ball.

Looking through the frosty window, she watched the bus drive away. Mary turned and waved last of all, Esther's package in her hand, a white square in her bright red mittens. As she waited for Father, Esther felt the smooth pink paper she held under her coat. She would not be lonely now, ever. In her room she could practice softly. By spring she would be able to do anything that anybody did with jacks. Then she and Mary would sit in the sun as the little leaves came on the trees again, and the bright red maple buds. "Good!" Mary would say. "Good, Esther, good!"

Christmas Eve came and candles burned in the windows. As suppertime came, Esther was praying so hard inside herself, and listening so hard outside herself, that she could scarcely get the table laid. The fire was spitting cheerfully and the smell of good cooking filled the house. Snowflakes slipped along the window panes and settled on the sills, making it more cozy and warm and beautiful in the house than it ever seemed in good weather.

Father bowed his head over the food and said a long silent prayer. It was while he prayed that Esther heard

footsteps coming. Dan knew the very moment Father would be asking the blessing. He had chosen the best time in every way.

Father said "Amen" and lifted his head and listened.

"Who would be coming tonight?" Mother asked.

Father stood up. "Whoever it is, he must be asked to eat tonight," he said. Esther's heart was beating so fast she felt sure she was going to faint and fall off her chair. A knock. She had barely time to whisper once more, "And help Father to remember the story about the Prodigal Son . . ."

Father opened the door. He stood without moving, then, with his hand still on the knob.

"Daniel!" Mother paid no attention to Father at all. She rushed past him as if he were not there. She opened her arms and held Dan close to her heart. "I have prayed for this day," she said. Her face was wet with tears and her dress with snow when she turned to the room again.

"Shall I come in, Father?" Dan asked, for Father still stood where he was, holding the door. Cold had swept into the room and a puff of snow blew over the bare floor. Suddenly Father let go of the door and leaned forward toward Dan as if he must lean upon him. He looked like an old, old man.

Esther saw that his eyes were filled with tears.

"It is Christmas," he said. "Come in."

When he came back to the table the tears had disappeared. His face looked strong and long and sober, like the picture of an apostle in the Bible. "Come and eat with us," he said simply. "Supper is ready."

Neither Father nor Mother seemed to notice for a while that Dan and Esther had not greeted each other. Esther had been too excited to move from her chair. But as Mother brought a fresh platter of chicken, she looked at Esther for the first time since Dan came in. All of her looking had been busy on him before.

"Well, aren't you glad to see your brother at home, Esther?" she asked. "Daniel, what do you think of our great girl? She will soon be as tall as I am."

Dan's eyes were laughing when he turned to look at Esther. Nobody else could see his face just then, so he gave her a solemn wink. He looked like the old Dan now, with his hair down below his ears and his collar high. She could see the familiar line of suspenders over his shoulders, under his open coat.

"Well, Esther, you have changed since I saw you last!" he said.

"And you also," she said politely.

"Many things have changed," he said. His look said to her, clearly, *And many things must go on changing in order for us to have one day and then another day. Today will be tomorrow. . . .*

Father seemed to have forgotten he had prayed over the food already. He bowed his head and prayed again for a long long time. Esther looked at Dan through the fingers she held over her face. Suddenly he too opened his eyes. They smiled at each other. It was their secret. They would have many, many more.

Then they both closed their eyes again until Father said "Amen."